GREAT ANIMAL ANTICS

2 BOOKS IN 1!

Katie Davies

Illustrated by Hannah Shaw

SIMON AND SCHUSTER

First published as an omnibus edition entitled *Great Animal Antics*
by Simon and Schuster UK Ltd, A CBS COMPANY
in Great Britain in 2011

The Great Hamster Massacre first published in Great Britain in 2010
by Simon and Schuster UK Ltd

The Great Rabbit Rescue first published in Great Britain in 2010
by Simon and Schuster UK Ltd

Simon & Schuster UK Ltd
1st Floor, 222 Gray's Inn Road, London WC1X 8HB

This book is a work of fiction. Names, characters, places and incidents are either the
product of the author's imagination or are used fictitiously. Any resemblance to actual
people living or dead, events or locales is entirely coincidental.

A CIP catalogue record for this book is available from the British Library.

978-0-85707-552-9

1 3 5 7 9 10 8 6 4 2

Printed and bound by CPI Group (UK) Ltd, Croydon, CR0 4YY

www.simonandschuster.co.uk
www.katiedaviesbooks.com

THE GREAT HAMSTER MASSACRE

Katie Davies

Illustrated by Hannah Shaw

SIMON AND SCHUSTER

For Daniel

A big thank you to my Mum and Dad, and my husband, Alan, and my agent, Clare Conville, for all their help.

❝ CHAPTER 1 ❞
What A Massacre Is

This is a story about me, and Tom, and our Investigation into the Hamster Massacre. I'm supposed to be writing my What-I-Did-In-The-Summer-Holidays Story for school, but I'm going to write this story first because you should always write a Real Investigation up straight away. That's what my friend Suzanne says. And Suzanne knows everything about Real Investigations. Mum said she didn't think my teacher would like the story of my real summer holidays, and how the Hamster Massacre happened.

She said, 'Anna (that's my name), *some* nice things must have happened this holidays and if you can't remember any, you can make some nice things up, and put them in your summer holiday report instead.'

Mum doesn't think it matters if my holiday report isn't exactly true, but Graham Roberts got in trouble last time when he put that he spent the whole holiday in the dog-basket. His dog had died, so maybe he *did* stay in the dog-basket all holiday, but Mrs Peters said he must have come out to eat and go to the toilet and things like that, and Joe-down-the-road told Tom he saw Graham at Cubs. And you can't be in a dog basket *there*.

Tom is my little brother. I've got another brother too, and a sister, but they're older than me and Tom and they don't really care about hamsters much, so they're not in this story. Tom is four years younger than me, except for a little while every year after he has his birthday, and before I have mine, when he is only *three* years younger. But most of the time he's four years younger, so it's best to say that.

Anyway, me and Tom are not supposed to talk about the hamsters and what happened to them anymore because it's best to try to forget about it all, and stop exaggerating, and making it worse than it actually was, and all that. But we couldn't do that anyway because massacres can't really get any worse than they are. That is the point of them.

This is what it says about massacres in my dictionary...

massacre [mass-a-ker] ✦ *noun*
a general slaughter of persons or animals:
'the massacre of millions during the war'

The dictionary in Suzanne's house said you could have another kind of massacre. It said...

massacre [mass-a-ker] ✦ *informal*
a bad defeat, especially in sport: 'England was massacred 5-0 by France in the semi-final'

But the Hamster Massacre was not that kind of massacre. The Hamster Massacre was definitely a *formal* kind of massacre.

I will keep the story of the Hamster Massacre in the shed with the worms, and the wasp trap, and the pictures that we traced from Joe-down-the-road's Mum's book. Me and Suzanne have made a lock for the shed door, and we've got a new password. We are the only ones allowed in the shed, except when we let Tom in, but he gets bored when we are making the locks and deciding on the passwords and stuff, and he is too little for the pictures from Joe's Mum's book so, most of the time, when we go in the shed, Tom goes in the house and has a biscuit.

👏 CHAPTER 2 👏
The Wall And The Window

Suzanne lives next door. Her surname is Barry.
The wall between our house and the Barrys'
house is thin. We can hear the Barrys through
the wall. We hear them when they scrape their
plates, and when they flush the loo, and we hear
their Dad shout,

'YOU BETTER GET DOWN THESE STAIRS BEFORE I HAVE TO COME UP!'

Mum says, imagine what the Barrys can hear
from our house. But none of the Barrys heard
anything unusual the day the massacre happened.

Last summer holidays, me and Suzanne made a plan for getting through the wall. Our bedrooms are right next to each other so, if I made a hole on my side of the wall, under my bed, and Suzanne made a hole in exactly the same place on her side of the wall, under her bed, the two holes would meet in the middle to make a tunnel. We wrote the plan on the back of a roll of wallpaper in the shed. Suzanne made a list of all the tools we needed, and I drew the diagrams with arrows on.

PLAN FOR GETTING THROUGH THE WALL

Tools
Big hammer
← Shovel
← Trowel
← Torch

My bed

HOLE

suzanne's bed

When we had finished, Suzanne wanted to do the diagrams again because she is a better drawer than I am, and then we fell out, so I took all the tools and hid them, and then Suzanne took the plan and hid that.

And Suzanne's Dad found the plan, and he looked under Suzanne's bed, and he saw that the paint had been picked off the wall, and that a hole had been made in the plaster, and now me and Suzanne aren't allowed to play in Suzanne's room **'EVER AGAIN!'**

I don't ring on the Barrys' doorbell if Suzanne's Dad is at home.

Anyway, we don't need a tunnel anymore because we've got a Knocking Code. This is how it works. When I go to bed, I knock three times on my bedroom wall and, if the coast is clear,

Suzanne knocks back three times, and then we both go to our windows and we open them and crawl out and sit outside on the ledge in the night.

Suzanne knows the names of all the stars like The Plough and Orion's Belt, and how to spot them, but she always points to a different place, and I never see anything that looks like a plough. I just say that I can.

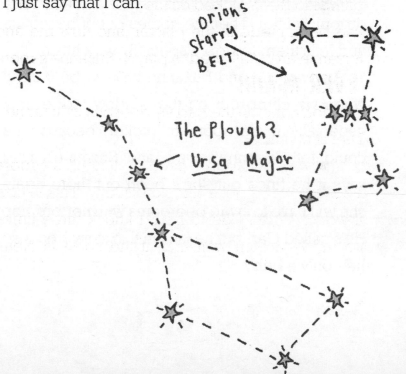

Sometimes we see Mr Tucker opposite standing by his window too. Mr Tucker's got a lot of medals from The War. He is easier to spot than The Plough. Normally, when Mr Tucker's at his window, he's looking out for people doing things he doesn't like, like burgling, or fighting, or dropping litter. Then he comes out of his house and tells them to stop. Especially if it's litter.

Anyway, me and Suzanne have to be careful when we climb out on the window ledge now, especially if we spot Mr Tucker, because he could tell Suzanne's Dad, and Suzanne's Dad says if he finds out she's been out there again she will have to swap bedrooms with her brother. He's called Carl but he isn't in this story because he's only a baby.

⚬ CHAPTER 3 ⚬
The New Cat

Before me and Tom got the hamsters, there were a lot of reasons why we weren't allowed to have any. The first reason was the cat. Our cat is not an ordinary cat that sits by the fire and lets you stroke her, and that is because she is from a farm where she was a Wild Cat. We used to have another cat and it was a much better one. But it got run over by Miss Matheson in the back lane. Miss Matheson doesn't like it if you go in her bit of the back lane. She says, **'PRIVATE PROPERTY! PRIVATE PROPERTY!'** And bangs on the window.

Miss Matheson never admitted that she ran

over the Old Cat but me and Tom know it was her because it was outside her house. And anyway, Suzanne saw cat blood on Miss Matheson's car tyres.

Before she got run over, the Old Cat used to let you do anything. You could wrap her in a blanket, put a hat on her, put her in a pram, and walk her down the road and she didn't even miaow.

You couldn't put the New Cat in a pram. You can't put the New Cat in anything, not even in its own basket, unless you've got gardening gloves on.

I bet Miss Matheson wishes she never killed the Old Cat because when it isn't hunting, or asleep with one eye open, the New Cat spends its time walking slowly up and down in front of Miss Matheson's gate. And it drives her dog mad.

Miss Matheson asked Mum if we could keep the cat inside but you can't keep the New Cat anywhere.

The New Cat hunts. Its bowl is always full of cat food, *special* cat food from small silver tins that the Old Cat only used to get at Christmas, but it still hunts. It hunts birds, mice, and Joe-down-the-road's New Rabbit.

It tried to hunt Joe's Old Rabbit too but as soon as it saw our New Cat, Joe's Old Rabbit panicked, and died.

Joe's Mum's Boyfriend looked at Joe's Old Rabbit and said, **'Heart attack. I'll get a trowel.'**

And he did, and he dug a hole in the back lane, and he put the Old Rabbit in the hole.

Joe didn't like seeing the soil go on the Old Rabbit's fur because when it was alive the Old Rabbit was very fussy about its fur, and it hated getting anything on it, and when it *did* get anything on it, like soil, or bits of carrot, it cleaned it off straight away.

I thought the Old Rabbit would rather have been put in a shoebox on some straw, with a dandelion, before it got put in the hole, but Joe's Mum's Boyfriend told me to be quiet.

Joe cried a lot because of the soil, and the fur, and because he wasn't allowed to even wipe it away from the Old Rabbit's eyes or mouth. And he knew the Old Rabbit would hate it.

Me and Suzanne told Joe that as soon as his Mum's Boyfriend went home, and stopped staying at his house, we would dig the Old Rabbit up, and clean its fur, and put it in a box, and make a cross to go in the ground behind it, like the Old Cat has.

But Joe kept on crying,
'GET THE SOIL OUT HIS EYES...
GET THE SOIL OUT HIS EYES...'
and his Mum's Boyfriend sent us home.

Anyway, when there aren't any birds or mice outside, and Joe is guarding his New Rabbit with a Super Soaker, and Miss Matheson won't let her dog in the garden, and the New Cat is sick of hunting spiders, and stones, and the wind, it sometimes wants to come in the house.

The New Cat doesn't stop hunting once it's inside the house and has finished fighting with the cat flap, either. Its best things for hunting inside the house are feet. It likes bare feet best, then in socks, then in slippers. If all the feet in the house are in shoes, and it is raining outside, it will also hunt the hoover, the spider plants and the sound of the Barrys' loo flushing.

Mum said that wherever we might put a hamster, in whatever kind of a cage, with however many guards, if the New Cat couldn't scare it to death she would hunt it and kill it in some other way.

She said, 'You and your brother may as well kill a hamster yourselves as bring one within a mile of the New Cat.'

I can't remember every single other reason why we weren't allowed the hamsters before we got them, but I know that the New Cat was Reason Number One.

CHAPTER 4
Reasons And Real Reasons

A lot of times, when someone tells you a reason why you can't have something, the reason isn't really true. Like when Mum tells Tom he can't have a Two Ball Screwball from the Ice Cream Man because the Ice Cream Man hasn't got any left. That reason isn't true. The *real* reason is that Two Ball Screwballs have got bubblegum in, and Tom is too young for bubblegum. Last time he had some he squished it in the bath mat.

Out of all the reasons for why somebody can't have something, being too young is the worst, so when 'too young' is the real reason, Mum mostly makes another one up instead.

Other times, when someone tells you a reason why you can't have something, the reason might be true, but it still might not be the real reason why they don't want you to have it. Like when Suzanne's Dad told Suzanne that she couldn't have any pets because he was allergic to pet hair. That's true, Suzanne's Dad *is* allergic to pet hair. It makes his nose run and his eyes itch and his face go red. And that's why the Barrys had to send their dog Barney to live on a farm. But it isn't the *real* reason why he won't let Suzanne have any pets. The real reason is because he *hates* pets. It was Tom who found that out.

In our house, Tom gets told more reasons for why he can't have things than anyone else. So all Tom does, whenever he gets told a reason, is think of something else he wants as fast as he can instead. So, when me and Suzanne told Tom all about how Suzanne wasn't allowed any pets because her Dad was allergic to pet hair, Tom said, 'What about a tortoise? They don't have hairs on.'

Suzanne thought about all the pets she'd asked for. A dog, a cat, a rabbit, a guinea pig, a hamster and a budgie (a budgie doesn't have hair exactly but her Dad said he is allergic to feathers too) and she hadn't ever even *asked* for a pet without hair like a tortoise.

So we thought of some pets that don't have hair on and we started to make a list.

ANNA'S AND TOM'S AND SUZANNE'S LIST OF PETS WITH NO HAIRS ON THAT SUZANNE'S DAD WON'T BE ALLERGIC TO

1. Tortoise
2. Frog
3. Snake
4. Stick Insect
5. Eel
6. Fish
7. Terrapin (a small tortoise that likes water)
8. Lizard

We couldn't think of any more pets with no hair on, so we went on the computer and we put 'pets with no hairs' in, and guess what? You can get dogs and cats and rabbits and guinea pigs and rats and hamsters and every single kind of pet there is without any hair on if you want it. There was a cat with no hairs on called a Sphinx, like the statues in Egypt that we did at school with Mrs Peters, and there were five kinds of dogs with no hairs on called Hairless Dogs, each with their own special name. Some of them are too hard to say, and they probably aren't even in English, but I'll write them down anyway.

HAIRLESS DOGS

1. Peruvian Inca Orchid
2. Hairless Chinese Crested
3. Hairless Khalla
4. American Hairless Terrier
5. Xoloitzcuintli

When Suzanne's Mum came to make her go home, we showed her the Hairless Dogs List and the pictures on the computer. When she saw the first ones she screamed and said 'Ugh! They look like aliens!' But when she saw the one called American Hairless Terrier, she said, 'Oh', and she looked sad and put her head on one side and said, 'That's the same kind of dog as Barney.'

It didn't look like Barney to me. But Suzanne's Mum said it was 'exactly like Barney. But bald.' My Mum said a bald dog was better than no dog, and Suzanne's Mum said, 'Same with men' and Suzanne's Mum and My Mum laughed a lot then, for ages, even though it isn't that funny. My Dad is bald. So is Suzanne's.

Suzanne's Mum said to Suzanne that if it was okay with her Dad, they could get a bald dog.

It wasn't okay with Suzanne's Dad, though, because we heard him shouting through the wall. He shouted louder than ever,

'I DON'T CARE ABOUT THE HAIR...'

He said,

'I JUST HATE PETS!'

And everyone went quiet because you can't ask, 'What about a tortoise?' after a reason like that.

CHAPTER 5
Hamster Horror

Although the New Cat was always Reason Number One for us not being allowed a hamster, it turned out not to be the real reason after all.

One night, after tea, when me and Tom didn't eat our onions and we had go to our rooms until we were ready to say sorry to Mum for making sick noises, we got thinking about hamsters, and how it was all the New Cat's fault that we weren't allowed to have one. So we made a plan, and we went downstairs where Mum was watching telly with Nanna.

And I said, *'We are sorry about the onions, Mum.'*

25

Mum didn't say anything because 'Coronation Street' was on and, even though she says she doesn't even like 'Coronation Street', and only puts it on for Nanna, she never likes talking when it's on.

Anyway, Tom said, 'Could we have a hamster if the New Cat was dead, or didn't live at our house for a different reason?'

Mum said, 'Mmm… what?' and then she said, 'No!'

And Tom said, 'Why?', which is Tom's favourite question.

And Mum said, 'Because. New Cat or no New Cat, hamsters are bad news.'

And Tom said, 'Why?' again.

And Mum said, 'Because.'

And then she said, 'Bed.'

And Tom said, 'Why?'

And Mum said, 'Right!'
And she stopped watching
'Coronation Street' and she
stood up and said, 'Ten…
Nine… Eight…'

And, then Nanna
said, 'Quick, go on up,
Duck, and I'll come
up too, and I'll tell you
a story.'

And Tom said 'Is it
about hamsters?'

And Nanna said, 'Yes, it is. It's all about what
happened to two little hamsters your Mum knew,

and why they were both bad news.'

Mum had never told us anything about knowing any hamsters, so we ran up and got ready as quickly as we could, and Tom let me brush his teeth, because he takes ages when he does it himself, and he doesn't even brush really, he just eats the toothpaste, and we got in Tom's bed and we waited for Nanna. Which took quite a long time because of Nanna's hips, and the stairs, and because Mum had to help her.

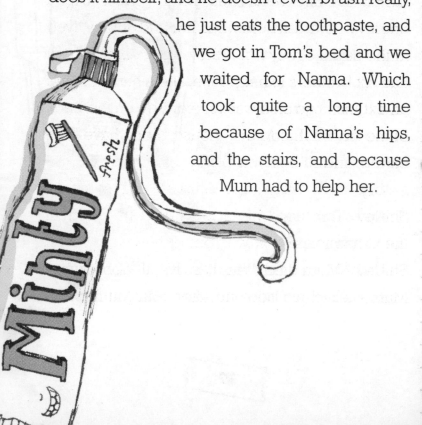

CHAPTER 6
Geoff And The Sliding Double Doors

The first hamster Nanna told us all about was called Geoff. Geoff was Mum's best friend Shirley's hamster, from when her and Shirley lived in the same street when they were girls. Shirley had six brothers in her house, and a hamster, and an extension, which was an extra bit on the back of the house that Mum's house didn't have. The extension had double sliding doors.

One day, Mum and Shirley and some of Shirley's brothers were playing with Geoff in the extension. Geoff was out of his cage, which Shirley's Mum didn't mind as long as Shirley and Mum picked his poos up after, and put them in the bin before Shirley's tea was ready.

But Shirley's youngest brother kept picking up Geoff's poos too, and chasing Mum and Shirley with them, and Mum and Shirley were screaming, and running in and out of the double sliding extension doors to escape from him, and Shirley's youngest brother was chasing them, and Mum and Shirley were screaming even more, and sliding the doors shut on Shirley's youngest brother as quickly as they could. And Geoff was running around too, because that's what hamsters do when they're allowed out of their cages.

And Mum ran towards the sliding doors and screamed and slid them open, and Shirley's brother ran after her. And Mum ran through the sliding doors into the garden, and screamed, and slid them shut.

And when she slid them shut she heard another little scream, from low down, and she looked to see what it was, and there, on *her* side of the door, in the garden, was the *front* half of Geoff. And she looked through the sliding doors, and there, on the *other* side of the door, in the extension, was the *back* half of Geoff. And the sliding doors were shut tight in-between.

CHAPTER 7
Bernard And The Cashmere Coat

The second hamster Nanna told us all about was called Bernard. Bernard was a big fat orange hamster with tiny black eyes that Dad bought Mum for her 21st birthday. Mum didn't really want a hamster for her 21st birthday but Dad bought her one because Shirley had told him all about how Mum had cut Geoff in half with the sliding doors when they were little girls, and how sad she had been, and Dad thought that maybe now she was grown up it would be funny if he bought her a hamster of her own.

Anyway, what Mum *really* wanted for her birthday was a green cashmere coat. She had seen the coat in the shops when she was in town with Shirley. It was the most beautiful, and the most green, and the most expensive coat that Mum and Shirley had ever seen, and Mum showed it to Dad every time they went past it.

← GREEN
+
EXPENSIVE

The night before Mum's birthday Dad told Mum that he had bought her a birthday present that was 'lovely and soft and warm', and Mum was sure it was the cashmere coat.

In the morning, when Dad gave Mum a big fat orange hamster, Mum was not very pleased. But she thought that, seeing as Dad had given her a hamster, she had better call it something. So she called it Bernard. And she put its cage on the table in the kitchen, and she started doing lots of tidying and cleaning because she was having a birthday party that night.

When everything was nearly ready Mum took Bernard's cage off the table because Bernard looked like the least clean and tidy thing in the house, and she put Bernard's cage on the shelf under the coat hooks in the cupboard under the stairs. She looked at Bernard and thought, 'He's very nice really', and she remembered how much she liked Geoff, before she killed him by mistake, and she thought how nice it would be to have a hamster after all. She took Bernard out of his cage and she stroked him on his back, and he *was* very lovely, and very soft and very warm, and she kissed him on the head, and she put him back in the cage and she shut the cupboard door. And then the doorbell rang, and Mum went to answer it, and it was Shirley. She was wearing the green cashmere coat! She had walked past the shop that morning, and bought it half price in the sale.

35

Shirley looked very nice in the coat. And Mum thought how nice *she* would have looked in it if it was *her* coat. Dad and Shirley laughed when Mum told them how she had thought Dad was getting her the coat for her birthday, and then he had given her a hamster. And Mum laughed too, but only a bit, because she didn't think it was all that funny. And she took Shirley's beautiful green cashmere coat, and she hung it up in the cupboard on the hooks above Bernard's cage.

When the party was over and it was time for everyone to go home, Mum went into

HAPPY BIRTHDAY

the cupboard to get everyone's coats. She took down Shirley's green cashmere coat and was just thinking how beautiful, and how green, and how soft it was, when she noticed that in the back of the coat, just where Shirley's bum would be if she was wearing it, there was a hole.

She didn't remember the hole being there when she hung the coat up, and she was just wondering how it might have got there since, when she saw something in Bernard's cage. Right there, in the middle of the cage, was a very beautiful, very green, very soft-looking nest.

uh oh

She lifted up the top of the nest, and she

screamed,
'ARGHHHH, BERNARD!!!'

He was lying on his back in the middle of the nest with his legs in the air, his little black eyes fixed and bulging, and his mouth, which was wide open, was full of very beautiful, very green, very expensive cashmere coat.

'And that,' said Nanna, 'was the end of Bernard. And *that* is why your Mum said she would "never, ever have another hamster". Because hamsters are all Bad News.'

And then Nanna gave us a kiss. Her kiss smelled like her talcum powder. And she turned out the light. And I stayed in Tom's bed because, like Nanna said, you don't have to stay in your own bed if it's the holidays.

❧ CHAPTER 8 ❧
Ask And It Shall Be Given

Most of the time, if you ask Mum for something a lot, especially if you follow her around and do it in a voice that goes, '**Oh PLeeEAse, Mum... PLeeEAse...**' in the end she will say, 'Oh, for Goodness sake, alright.'

But not this time. Not with the hamster. Even with Tom asking, 'Why?'

And,

'What about if it's a very small hamster?'

Or,

'What about if we never let it out?'

Or,

'What about if we make it sleep in the garden?'

Mum just said, 'No' and put the hoover on, and turned the radio right up. So we decided to ask Suzanne to do a plan for getting a hamster with us.

We knocked on the wall three times and then we waited for a bit. Suzanne didn't knock back so either the coast wasn't clear, or she didn't hear us knocking because she was asleep, or maybe she was downstairs having her breakfast. So we knocked another three times, and waited again, and she still didn't knock back, so we knocked as hard as we could for a long time and then Suzanne's Dad opened the window very fast with his dressing gown on and he leaned out and shouted, **'FOR CRYING OUT LOUD, STOP BANGING ON THE WALL! AND RING ON THE DOORBELL LIKE A NORMAL HUMAN BEING!'**

I didn't want to ring on the doorbell like a normal human being so Tom went instead, and he told Suzanne we were doing a plan.

Suzanne came round, and she brought all her pens, and we made a new password for the day for Shed Club. It took quite a long time because Tom wanted the password to be 'Tom' and Suzanne said that was too easy.

And I wanted the password to be 'Hamster Plan' and Suzanne said if anyone heard it they would know that we were making a plan about a hamster.

And Suzanne wanted the password to be 'Rabbit', and I said the plan was about hamsters, not rabbits, so why should that be the password? But Suzanne said if the password wasn't 'Rabbit' she was going home, and she was taking her pens with her. So that was what it was.

After we decided on the password, Tom went in the house for a biscuit, and Suzanne started thinking of all the things that I could do to get a hamster. And I started writing them all down. We did two lists. And this is what they said…

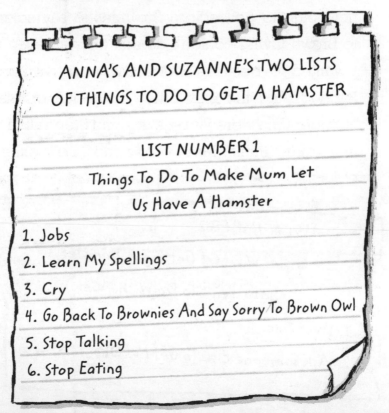

ANNA'S AND SUZANNE'S TWO LISTS OF THINGS TO DO TO GET A HAMSTER

LIST NUMBER 1

Things To Do To Make Mum Let
Us Have A Hamster

1. Jobs
2. Learn My Spellings
3. Cry
4. Go Back To Brownies And Say Sorry To Brown Owl
5. Stop Talking
6. Stop Eating

The thing was, I had already done most of the things that Suzanne thought of to put in List Number One. I had tried Jobs and I had tried to Learn My Spellings and I had tried Crying. Mum said I couldn't have a hamster but if I carried on crying she would give me an Oscar. And I was not going to go back to Brownies to say sorry to Brown Owl. I couldn't do that anyway, even if I wanted to, because Brown Owl said that I am Banned. And the only other things left on List Number One were Stop Eating, and Stop Talking, and I didn't think Mum would mind if I did either of those.

LIST NUMBER 2

Other Ways Of Getting A Hamster
That Aren't To Do With Mum

1. Steal One

2. Ask Someone Else To Get Me One

The first thing on List Number Two was steal a hamster. I didn't really want to steal anything again if I could help it because the last time I stole something Mum made me take it back, and she said she had half a mind to tell Nanna's friend Mrs Rotherham up the road on me because Mrs Rotherham used to be in the police. And then I would have to go to The Young Offenders' Institution, which is a jail, but for children, and I definitely wouldn't be allowed to have a hamster there. Me and Tom always used to run when we went past Mrs Rotherham's house.

The only other thing that was left on the list was to Ask Someone Else To Get Me One. Suzanne said I should ask My Dad. It's different with My Dad than Suzanne's Dad though, because if you ask My Dad something he never says 'Yes' or 'No', he only says, 'Ask your mother. She's in charge.'

And then Mum says she is not in charge, and if she *was* in charge, Dad would be clearing out all of his rubbish from the cupboard under the stairs, like she has been asking him to do for the last ten years, instead of drinking beer and watching the football, and then she says, **'And NO. For the last time, you cannot have a hamster!'**

So we tried to think of someone else to ask to get me a hamster who was in charge of Mum. And the only person we could think of was Nanna.

Nanna stayed at our house a lot because of her hips, and needing help, and things like that. And some of the time when she came to our house she had to stay in bed. And then Nanna really liked it if we went into her room to ask her if she wanted anything. Normally she only wanted you to sit on the bed with her, which Mum said we could, as long as Nanna wasn't asleep. This time Nanna was asleep, but I went in to ask her if she wanted anything anyway because then I could ask her if she would get me a hamster. It took ages trying to ask Nanna because first she had to wake up, and then she had to put her hearing aid in, and then she couldn't turn it on, and it kept squeaking, and in the end she said I should just shout because she couldn't make the hearing aid work.

So I did. I tried shouting to ask if she wanted me to get her anything first, but she still couldn't hear, so in the end I just shouted as loud as I could, *'CAN. I. HAVE. A. HAMSTER?'*

Nanna laughed. I didn't laugh because I didn't think it was funny.

And then Nanna said, 'Ah, I'm sorry, Duck, hop up.' And she patted the bed. Nanna's bed smelled like her talcum powder. Nanna said, 'If I was in charge, I'd let you have ten hamsters, Duck. But I'm not, I'm sorry.'

And she cuddled me in, and stroked me on the head until she fell asleep again.

I went back to the shed and told Suzanne what Nanna said about not being in charge. And I said that maybe we should go and dig up Joe-down-the-road's Old Rabbit instead, because none of the plans for getting a hamster were working. But Suzanne had thought of another person to ask for a hamster, someone who Mum wasn't in charge of, and that person was God.

CHAPTER 9
Our Father...

Sometimes, on Sundays, Mum and Nanna go to Church, and me and Tom go to Sunday School in the cottage next door to the Church, because children aren't allowed to be in Church for long in case they start laughing or crying or needing a wee. You can't do those kinds of things in Church. The only things you *can* do in Church are kneeling

on the cushions and saying the Amens. Unless you are Confirmed, and then you can eat the Body Of Christ and drink His Blood.

But me and Tom aren't old enough to do that, so we go to Sunday School instead and just go into Church for the last bit at the end.

You can do most things in Sunday School, like colouring and singing and dressing up, as long as you don't dress up as Jesus on the cross, because Graham Roberts did that once, just in his pants, and Mrs Constantine didn't like it.

Mrs Constantine is in charge of Sunday School, and she is the Vicar's Wife.

Anyway, when Sunday School is finished you do the Prayer, and have a biscuit, and then everyone from Sunday School goes into Church for the last bit and sits with their Mums. Sometimes they sit with their Dads as well, but mostly they sit with their Mums because not many Dads go to Church.

Our Dad doesn't go. He doesn't even believe in God. Graham Roberts said Dad will probably go to Hell. Nanna said Dad won't go to Hell and Graham Roberts shouldn't say things like that because he doesn't know what he is talking about.

There aren't very many children in Sunday School. Sometimes it's ten, and sometimes it's six, and once it was only two, and that was when it was just me and Tom, and then Mrs Constantine said there wasn't any point in even doing Sunday School that week, and she made me and Tom go into Church for the whole time with Mum and Nanna. And that was when we got in Big Trouble because we had The Hysterics because first everyone in Church had to shake hands with each other and say, 'Peace be with you', and the lady who was sitting behind Tom kept saying '*Peath* Be With You' instead. And then the Vicar said 'Hymn 97' and that's the hymn that goes…

> I was cold. I was naked.
> Were you there?
> Were you there?
> I was cold. I was naked.
> Were you there?

And me and Tom kept thinking about when Graham Roberts was Jesus, just in his pants. And then the lady who was sitting behind us who had said 'Peath Be With You' hit Tom hard on the head with her Hymn Book.

And then we *really* got The Hysterics. And we had to lie on the floor under the pew.

Nanna asked the Peath Be With You Lady if she would mind *not* hitting Tom on the head with her Hymn Book.

But the Peath Be With You Lady said she would very much mind not hitting Tom on the head with her Hymn Book, because Tom was Out Of Control and children like us had 'No buithneth being in Church'.

And Nanna said, 'Suffer the little children' which is something from in the Bible that Jesus said which means you can't really hit children on the head with your Hymn Book or anything, even if they *have* got The Hysterics.

The Peath Be With You Lady said, **'Thuffer nothing. They've ruined the thurvith.'**

And then Nanna had to leave the Church because she said she had a bad cough, but really it was because she had The Hysterics a bit too.

53

And she took me and Tom with her and we went to get an ice cream, even though it was raining, because Nanna said ice cream is good for calming down.

●꞉ ●꞉ ●꞉

But we didn't get The Hysterics when we went to Church to ask God about having a hamster.

Mum didn't want to go to Church that day because Nanna was staying in bed with her hips. But we promised we wouldn't get The Hysterics and, in the end, Mum said 'alright then' because, when you ask to go to Church, it's not really the kind of thing that a Mum can say 'No' to. Not like when you ask to go to Alton Towers or something like that.

And Suzanne said she wanted to come along too because she had never been to Church before.

In the morning, before we left, Mum said we should go and give Nanna a kiss and tell her we were going to Church because she would like that. Maybe she did like it but she didn't open her eyes. I gave Nanna a kiss on the cheek, and so did Suzanne, and Tom gave her a kiss on the hand because he doesn't like kissing Nanna on the cheek because he says she prickles, which she does, but only a little bit. Nanna's cheek smelled like her talcum powder. Suzanne said our Nanna looked very small in the bed, which she did, because she hardly made a shape under the covers, but the bed is quite big so that

55

probably made her look smaller.

Mrs Constantine was pleased that we had brought a new person to Sunday School and she was even more pleased when she asked Suzanne what she would like to do and Suzanne said 'I need to ask God for something'.

Mrs Constantine told Suzanne that, 'asking God for something is called praying'. Which Suzanne already knew, but she pretended she didn't. Mrs Constantine gave Suzanne a Bible, and she showed her which page told you how to do praying. It was quite hard to read, so Mrs Constantine read it first. She said, 'But thou, when thou prayest, enter into thy closet, and when thou hast shut thy door, pray to thy Father which is in secret; and thy Father which seeth in secret shall reward thee openly. . .

After this manner therefore pray ye:

> Our Father which art in heaven,
> Hallowed be thy name.
> Thy kingdom come.
> Thy will be done, In earth, as it is in heaven.
> Give us this day our daily bread.
> And forgive us our trespasses,
> As we forgive those who trespass against us.
> Lead us not into temptation,
> But deliver us from evil:
> For thine is the kingdom,
> The power and the glory,
> For ever and ever.
> A-men.'

Suzanne said, 'Thank you' to Mrs Constantine, and she took the Bible.

We waited until Mrs Constantine wasn't looking, and then me and Tom and Suzanne

57

snuck up the stairs, where you aren't supposed to go, into the store room where there is a big cupboard, which is almost a closet, where all the old Bibles are, and the Hymn Books, and the purple cloths, and the gold crosses and things like that, because that was the best place to do it.

It was pretty dark inside the old cupboard, once you got right in. I wanted Suzanne and Tom to come in the cupboard with me, but Suzanne said I had to go in on my own and close the door, and pray in secret like Mrs Constantine said.

I said the Prayer, the bits I could remember, because it was too dark to read, and then I said, 'Amen', and then I waited for a bit. And then, just to make sure, I said, 'Can I have a hamster?'

And then I said 'Please.'

And then I said 'Amen', again.

When I was finished, and I tried to get out of the cupboard, I couldn't find the door because it was too dark and I couldn't remember which side of the cupboard it was on. I shouted for Tom and Suzanne but they had gone back downstairs to do singing with the others. Tom always sings the loudest even though he doesn't know the words. I pushed, but the door didn't open. The cupboard was very dark and it smelled dusty, of old things and mothballs, like Nanna's house used to. And I could smell Nanna's talcum powder, as strong as if Nanna was there in the cupboard too.

I breathed in the smell as much as I could, until I thought I was going to sneeze, and I shouted,

'LET ME OUT!'

And then a spider, or a mouse, or a rat ran over my foot. So then I *really* wanted to get out of the cupboard. I am not scared of spiders and mice and rats and things because I quite like them, but I don't really like them running over my feet in a dark cupboard when I can't see. So I leaned on the door as hard as I could, and I screamed,

'HELP!'

And then the whole cupboard fell right over, and it crashed onto the floor with me inside.

Mrs Constantine ran upstairs and said 'Hello? Who's there?

And I said 'Me.'

And she said 'Who?'

And I said,

'ME! HELP! I'M IN THE CUPBOARD.'

But Mrs Constantine couldn't help because she couldn't lift the cupboard up because it was quite a heavy cupboard, even when I wasn't inside it, and I weigh five stones and two pounds, which is 28 kilograms, so she had to get the caretaker.

When I got out we all had a biscuit, and some juice, and looked for the rat, but we couldn't find it because it had got away, and then we went into Church for the last bit. And we stood at the back. And the Vicar said, 'Therefore I say unto you, what things soever ye desire, when ye pray, believe that ye receive them, and ye shall have them. For everyone that asketh receiveth; and he that seeketh findeth; and to him that knocketh it shall be opened. Or what man is there of you, whom if his son ask bread, will he give him a stone? Or if he ask a fish, will he give him a serpent?'

And Suzanne whispered, 'Or, if she ask for a hamster, will he give a rat?'

And Mrs Constantine said, 'Shh.'

And then we went to sit with Mum.

When we got home, Dad told me and Tom to wait downstairs while Mum went upstairs to see Nanna, but Tom went up anyway, and I followed after.

Mum was sitting on Nanna's bed. And Nanna was in it. Nanna looked even smaller in the bed than before. And Mum was crying.

Tom asked Mum if she was sad. Mum nodded her head.

Tom said, 'Why?' But Mum didn't answer because she put her hand over her mouth instead. And she patted the bed with her other hand.

And me and Tom got up. I could smell Nanna's talcum powder again. And Mum said that Nanna was dead. And she cried for a long time then, and she cuddled us in, and she stroked us on the head.

❝ CHAPTER 10 ❞

The Hamsters Came In Two By Two

After Nanna died, I decided I wouldn't ask Mum about a hamster again, and I wouldn't tell her how Nanna said if she was in charge she would let me have ten hamsters, or how I asked God for one, because Mum was sad quite a lot.

Then, the day after Nanna's funeral, Mum said we were going to a special shop.

Tom said, 'Has it got hamsters?'

And Mum said, 'Yes.'

The man in the shop had a brand new kind of hamster

cage that was round and made of plastic, and it had plastic tubes to go with it, which you could attach together to make tunnels. And the Pet Shop Man said that was the best kind of hamster cage you could get.

But Mum said we had only come in the shop to get one normal hamster, and she had already agreed to buy two Russian Dwarf hamsters, and an exercise-wheel, and a water bottle, and a book called *Hamsters: A Manual*. And we had a perfectly good cage at home in the cupboard under the stairs and Dad would just have to find it.

So the Pet Shop Man put the hamsters in a brown box with some sawdust and some air holes and we took the hamsters home in that.

When we got to the bottom of our road, Tom ran ahead to see if Dad had found the cage yet. Mr Tucker was in the road picking up litter, which he always does. And Tom was running up the road, and Mr Tucker was coming out of the hedge backwards, and he had some toilet paper in one hand, and a bin bag full of litter in his other hand, and there were lots of sticky-buds and twigs and things stuck to his tie and his blazer. And Tom was running his fastest, and he probably had his eyes shut, and Mr Tucker looked up and saw Tom coming and he said, 'Hallo, look keen! Let up!'

But Tom ran right into Mr Tucker, and Mr Tucker dropped the toilet paper and the bin bag full of litter and said, 'Oomph! Good God! What a belt!'

And Tom fell over on the gravel.

And Mr Tucker said, 'What's this arrival, eh? I could have done with an Arse-end Charlie there. I think that makes you an Ace, old chum.'

And Tom started crying.

And Mr Tucker said, 'Ah ha, frozen on the stick, eh? Well, where's your salute, Sir? You know the drill. On your feet. Look lively. Fling one up.'

And Tom got up and gave Mr Tucker the salute, even though he was crying, because it's one of Tom's best things to do when he sees Mr Tucker, and Mr Tucker gave him one back and he said, 'Smashing job. Good show, me old sawn-off. Where's that knee? Better have a quick shufti. Ooh, a humdinger. Dicey do, that was. You'll live, I'd say, but will you have to have the leg off?

What do you think?'

And Tom said, 'No', because he had stopped crying, and his knee was only bleeding a bit.

And Mr Tucker said, 'No? Quite right. That's the spirit. Press on regardless. You're not washed out yet. Plane's a write-off but you'll just have to wear it. Be glad you didn't land in the drink. In a bad way myself, as it goes. Got me in the goolies.'

And that made Tom laugh.

And Mr Tucker said, 'Hallo' to Mum.

And Mum said, 'Hello' to Mr Tucker.

And I didn't say anything because I didn't want to start talking to Mr Tucker in case it was about litter.

And then Mr Tucker said to Mum, 'Black do, your mother hopping the twig. Heard a buzz the old girl was low on juice. Clocked the blood wagon outside a week gone Sunday, thought "Hallo, look up," and a couple of body-snatchers bringing her in. Bad show all round. Beautiful blonde job like that. Doesn't do. Doesn't do.'

And Mum said, 'Thank you.'

And then Mr Tucker said, 'What do you say, Popsie? She was a fine woman, eh?'

And I said, 'Yes.'

And Mr Tucker said, 'A very fine woman.' And then he said, 'And she was flat out for me plugging away at this litter situation. Took a dim view of it, very dim, I can tell you. Last time I saw her she said to me, "Wing Commander", she said, "I think somebody, somewhere, is playing silly beggars with this litter." "Silly beggars," she said.'

And then Mr Tucker stared at me until Tom said, 'We've got hamsters.'

Mr Tucker pointed his finger at me, and closed one eye and said, 'Mmmmm.'

I didn't say anything to Mr Tucker but I don't

70

believe Nanna said anything about silly beggars because for one thing that wasn't really the kind of thing that Nanna did say, and if she *was* going to say it, she probably wouldn't say it to Mr Tucker because she didn't like talking about litter much either.

Mr Tucker said, 'Hamsters, Tom, is it? Where d'you get 'em?'

And Tom said, 'The pet shop.'

And Mr Tucker said, 'Pet shop, eh?'

And Tom said, 'Yes.'

And Mr Tucker said, 'How many?'

And Tom said, 'Two.'

Mr Tucker said, 'Two of 'em, eh?'

And Tom said, 'Yes.'

And Mr Tucker said, 'Smashing.'

And Tom said, 'Yes.'

And I was getting bored of listening to Tom and Mr Tucker so I said, 'They're from Russia.'

Mr Tucker said, 'Russia? Good God, Girl! Have you lost your wool completely?'

And I said how the man in the shop said that the Russian ones were the best.

Mr Tucker said, 'I'd take a lean view of that, my girl. I know a thing or two about the Russians. Slippery. Very slippery.'

And then Mr Tucker took the box with the hamsters in off me, and took the lid off, and the hamsters could have got out or anything.

But they didn't.

And Mr Tucker looked in the box and he said, 'Just as I thought. Couple of gremlins. What are you calling them?'

Tom said, 'Don't know.'

And Mr Tucker said, 'Number One, and Number Two, Basher. That's what I'd call 'em.'

And Tom said, 'I need a wee.'

Which he did because he was hopping from one foot to the other, and he had been doing it for ages, and that's what he does when he needs a wee.

So Mr Tucker gave Tom the salute.

And Tom gave Mr Tucker the salute back.

And Mr Tucker said, 'That's it. You've got the green, Old Chum. Chocks away.'

And then he made Tom's hair messy.

And then he looked at me and said, 'Silly

73

beggars… Mmmm.'

And then he went back into the hedge.

And me and Tom and Mum went into the house.

CHAPTER 11 👣

Housing The Hamsters

When we got in the house Dad had found the hamster cage and he'd cleaned it out, and put it in my room, and put some sawdust in it, and a food bowl. And Mum attached the water bottle and then she put the wheel in. The only thing with the hamsters was, because of them being Russian Dwarf hamsters, when we put them in the cage, their legs were too small to make the wheel go round, and their mouths were too small to get the water out of the bottle, and their bodies were too small to not be able to get out between the bars. And they did get out between the bars. And one of them weed on the carpet. And Mum started crying, and left the room, even though it was only a little wee. But Dad said Mum wasn't really crying about the wee, and not to worry.

Tom said, 'Is she crying about Nanna?'

And Dad said, 'Yes.'

And then Mum and Dad went into Nanna's room, and closed the door, and they changed Nanna's bed, and put her things in boxes. And afterwards it looked like nothing had ever happened.

Me and Tom cleaned up the wee on the carpet and we put the hamsters back in the brown box with the air-holes. And after that Mum went to bed.

Then Dad went to see Mrs Rotherham up

the road because she has got a lot of fish in her house, and he said maybe she had an old fish tank that we could borrow, and we could use that for a hamster cage instead. And Tom stayed in the house because he didn't want to go to Mrs Rotherham's because Mrs Rotherham used to be in the police, and Mum sometimes said she had half a mind to tell Mrs Rotherham on Tom when he was In Trouble, and Tom wasn't sure if she had or not. And I stayed in the house too because I needed to find out some things about the hamsters.

CHAPTER 12
From Russia With Love

This is what it said in my dictionary about Russians…

Russian [rush-un] ♦ *noun*
someone or something from Russia

And this is what it said in my dictionary about dwarfs…

dwarf [dworf] ♦ *noun*
a person of abnormally small stature
suffering from a bone growth disorder

I didn't think that the hamsters were suffering from anything, except maybe being in the box, so I went and knocked on Suzanne's wall to see what the dictionary said in her house. Suzanne isn't allowed to take the dictionary out of her house anymore because last time she took it, when we needed to look up some words from Joe-down-the-road's Mum's book in the shed, she forgot to take it back. And that was when I thought it would be a good lid for the worms.

It wasn't a very good lid for the worms because the next day the worms weren't really moving anymore. And then the dictionary got some of the worms' mud on it. And then Suzanne got in Big Trouble off her Dad, because he said, **'WHERE ON EARTH IS MY DICTIONARY, SUZANNE?'**

And Suzanne came to my house to get it, and we tried to get the mud off but it just made it worse, and then Mum said I had to go with Suzanne to take the dictionary back.

And then Suzanne's Dad said, **'WHAT IN GOD'S NAME HAVE YOU BEEN DOING WITH IT?'**

And I said about how I had been using it for a worm lid.

And Suzanne's Dad said, **'DOES IT _LOOK_ LIKE A**

WORM LID, FOR CRYING OUT LOUD?'

And then Suzanne's Dad said Suzanne was never allowed to take the dictionary, or anything else, out of his house again, because of Suzanne being,

'...INCAPABLE OF BEHAVING LIKE A NORMAL HUMAN BEING!'

I said that maybe Suzanne could go and get the dictionary anyway, because her Dad wasn't at home, and she could stay in her room with the dictionary, which wouldn't be taking it out of the house, and I could go on the window ledge, and she could read what it says about dwarfs through the window and I could write it down, and then she could put the dictionary straight back.

So that is what we did.

81

This is what it said about dwarfs in the dictionary in Suzanne's house...

dwarf [dworf] ✦ *noun*
a being in the form of a small mythical man, usually having magic powers

I didn't think the hamsters were men, because Mum asked the Pet Shop Man about ten times, and the Pet Shop Man said they were definitely both female. And I didn't think they had magic powers because I don't believe in that kind of thing anymore, because I am nine. Anyway, then the dictionary in Suzanne's house said...

dwarf [dworf] ✦ *noun*
of unusually small stature or size; diminutive. For example, dwarf star

The hamsters *were* unusually small, because that was how they got through the bars in the cage. Suzanne said she knew how to spot Dwarf Stars, and she said she would tell me all about them if I liked. But I said I had to go and check on the hamsters. And then Suzanne said she had got a new bike that used to be her cousin's, and I should come to her house and see it. But Dad came back with a new wheel that was smaller, and a water bowl, and a fish tank from Mrs Rotherham. So I said, 'I'll knock for you later' and I shut the window.

●? ●? ●?

We put the sawdust in the fish tank, and the new wheel, and the water bowl, and the food bowl, and some tissue paper for a nest, and then we put the hamsters in. The hamsters stood very still

83

in the middle of the fish tank. And then we looked in the book for what to do next. And Dad read it with us because it was quite hard to read.

"The Russian Dwarf, or Djungarian, Hamster, properly known as Phodopus Sungoris Campbelli and otherwise referred to as Campbell's Dwarf Hamster, or Hairy-Footed Dwarf Hamster, ought not to be confused with the Winter White, or Siberian, Hamster from the closely-related sub-species, Phodopus Sungorus."

Tom said he didn't like the book and he wanted to go and see Mum.

But Dad said he couldn't, and he gave Tom a whole packet of biscuits, chocolate ones, and then Tom said he didn't mind staying. So Dad read some more.

"The Russian Dwarf Hamster is a diminutive rodent, compact of body, with an undersized tail and, in common with all Cricetinae, expandable cheek pouches. The range of normal length of the Russian Dwarf lies between 60 and 113 millimetres (tail inclusive)."

We got a tape measure, and we measured the hamsters, which was quite hard because they didn't really like being measured. Hamster Number One was 56 millimetres long, and its tail was seven millimetres. And she was the Small One. Hamster Number Two was 62 millimetres long, and I couldn't measure its tail because it kept trying to bite me. But she was the Big One.

Anyway, then it said in the book…

"There are numerous variants and hybrids in terms of coat and colouring. Most commonly, the fur of the upper body is short, flat and greyish brown, with a white underside, and a dark brown stripe running the length of the spine. Such a variant is found in the wild, as well as domestically, and is properly referred to as the Agouti."

I didn't want to read the book anymore because it was hard to understand, and it didn't really help with what to do with hamsters, and Tom didn't want to read the book anymore either because he had finished the biscuits. So Dad went to go and find something to make a lid for the fish tank. And me and Tom gave the hamsters some sunflower seeds instead.

You can feed hamsters sunflower seeds for

ages because they just keep taking more and more and they stuff them in their cheeks until they look like they are going to burst and then (which is my best bit) they go into a corner and they push all the seeds out of their cheeks, and they bury them in the sawdust for eating later.

If you want, you can collect up the old seeds that have been in their cheeks after they've emptied them out, and you can give them back to the hamsters to put them in their cheeks again, and that means you don't have to buy millions of seeds all the time. It's not very nice when you put the old seeds back in because they're normally pretty soggy, and sometimes they're mixed in with other things they've put in their cheeks, and sometimes that can be poos.

I put some of the sunflower seeds on my hands and on my arms. And Hamster Number Two, which was the Big One, crawled along and put them in her cheeks. And then I put some sunflower seeds on Tom's arms, and on his shoulders, and some on the top of his head and Hamster Number Two ran all over him.

Tom didn't really like that, because Hamster Number Two was too fast, and he didn't like its feet, and it emptied all the soggy sunflower seeds out of its cheeks in Tom's hair. Tom said he liked Hamster Number One better because it was smaller and because it would sit still in your hand if you were very quiet, and it didn't mind being stroked if you gave it the crumbs from the biscuits.

88

And then the doorbell rang and it was Suzanne. I knew it was Suzanne because she did three rings. So I put the hamsters back in the fish-tank and I told Tom to watch them, and I went to the door.

Suzanne said, 'Are you coming out?'

And I said, 'No. I need to make an obstacle course for the hamsters. You could come in.'

But Suzanne said, 'No. I need to go on my bike. It's new.'

And I said, 'You can hold one of the hamsters.'

But Suzanne said, 'No. I don't want to. I'm probably allergic.'

I said, 'No, you're not.'

And Suzanne said, 'I could be. My Dad is. It might run in families.'

And I said, 'You're Dad's probably not allergic.

He's probably lying.'

And Suzanne said, 'My Dad's not a liar. *You're* a liar. You said you were going to knock on the wall for me later and you didn't.'

And then she said she was going to tell her Dad about how I made her get the dictionary. And she said she was going to call on Joe-down-the-road and ask him to come and play on bikes instead.

And I said, 'Good.' Because I said she probably loved Joe-down-the-road, and she was probably going to do all the things from Joe's Mum's book.

And Suzanne said, 'No. You are, and you've probably done them already.' And then she got on her bike and went away.

Sometimes I hate Suzanne.

● ● ●

I started doing the obstacle course and everything and then Suzanne came round to the back door. I knew it was Suzanne because she did three knocks.

When I opened the back door it was very loud because the bin lorry was there, collecting the rubbish. And Suzanne had to shout. She said, 'DO YOU WANT TO GO IN THE SHED AND MAKE A PLAN FOR DIGGING UP THE OLD RABBIT AND EVERYTHING AND I CAN BRING ALL MY PENS OVER AND CARD AND THINGS AND WE CAN MAKE A BOX?'

And I said, 'NO.' Because I was too busy with the hamsters.

And Suzanne said, 'DO YOU WANT TO LOOK AT MY BIKE?'

And I said, 'WHAT?' Because the Bin Lorry was getting louder because it was right by

Suzanne's back door.

And Suzanne said, 'MY BIKE!'

And I said, 'WHERE IS IT?'

And Suzanne said, 'THERE!'

And I said, 'WHERE?'

And Suzanne said, 'THERE! BY THE BINS!'

And she turned round and pointed to the bins. But her bike *wasn't* there because one of its wheels was sticking out of the bin lorry.

SUZANNE'S BIKE

And Suzanne screamed and ran to the Bin Man and said, '*GET IT OUT! THAT'S MY NEW BIKE!*'

But the teeth came down. There was a big crunch and a grinding noise.

And the Bin Man said, **'TOO LATE, LOVE. I'M NOT PSYCHIC! IF IT'S NOT FOR THE BIN LORRY, DON'T PUT IT BY THE BINS!'**

And he got in the bin lorry and drove off.

And Suzanne ran home.

And there was a lot of shouting in Suzanne's house because we heard it through the wall. And Suzanne cried a lot. Because of the bike. And the Bin Man. And her Dad. And because it wasn't her fault really.

And then, when it went quiet, she knocked on my wall three times.

93

And I opened my window.

And Suzanne opened her window and she said, 'I hate you.' And then she shut her window.

I didn't shut mine. I stayed on the window ledge for ages. There was a magpie in the garden, and I wanted to tell Suzanne because Nanna once told me and Suzanne that whenever you see a magpie you should always say, 'Hello, Mr Magpie. How's your wife and children?' because that stops you getting bad luck. And, since then, we always do. So I knocked on Suzanne's window. But Suzanne closed her curtains.

When I came in from the window ledge the New Cat was in my bedroom. It was crouched very low down. And its eyes were very wide. And its mouth was very open. And it was staring right at the hamsters.

` CHAPTER 13 `
The Birds And The Bees

Tom didn't look after the hamsters as much as me because sometimes he wanted to go outside and do other things, like hold the bin bag for the litter for Mr Tucker, or walk in a straight line with his eyes closed, or collect gravel. But I didn't want to go out at all because I didn't feel like it, and because Suzanne didn't want to be my friend anymore, and because if Suzanne decided she *did* want to be my friend again I knew that she would knock on the wall and, if I went out, I wouldn't hear her. So I stayed in my room on my own with the hamsters. And that's probably why I didn't notice that anything was different about

Number One. Because you don't really know that something is growing if you see it a lot. And that's why when you see a grown-up that you haven't seen for ages they say, 'Ooh, you've grown' but people who see you every day, like your Mum, don't say it because it happens too slowly for them to notice.

Tom said, 'Number One is fat.'

'No she isn't,' I said.

'Yes she is,' Tom said. 'She's fat. She's more fatter than Number Two.'

I looked at Number One, and I looked at Number Two. And Number One *was* fatter. A lot fatter.

'She used to be more skinnier,' Tom said.

I measured Number Two's tummy. She bit me. It was 76 millimetres around. And then I measured

Number One's tummy. It was 109 mm around. I decided to put Number One on a diet.

It was quite hard putting Number One on a diet because Number One and Number Two shared the same food bowl. So I took Number One out of the fish-tank when I fed Number Two. And I took Number Two out when I fed Number One. And I did that with gardening gloves on because of Number Two's biting.

I gave Number One half the amount of food that I gave Number Two. And I didn't give Number One any sunflower seeds. And I made sure that Number Two didn't put her sunflower seeds in her cheeks to hide for later, in case Number One found them and ate them all. Because even though *I* wouldn't eat something that had been in someone else's cheeks and spat back out again, hamsters aren't very fussy about things like that.

I measured Number One every day. But she didn't get any smaller. She just kept on getting bigger.

One afternoon Mum came into my room and Tom said, 'Number One is fat and she's getting even fatter. She's going to pop.'

Mum looked at Number One
and she said, 'Oh, please God, no.'
And she went downstairs to phone the Pet
Shop Man.

Me and Tom picked up the other phone in
Mum's room and listened in. We aren't allowed
to listen in on the other phone, because
Mum says it's rude, but sometimes we have to if
it's very important.

Mum said, 'I think one of the hamsters you
sold us is pregnant.'

Tom said, 'Oh!'

Mum said, 'Anna and Tom, I know you're there.
Put the phone down.'

We put the phone down. It was hard to be
quiet because if Number One *was* pregnant
that meant we would get a baby hamster.

In fact that meant we would get *lots* of baby hamsters because hamsters don't just have one or two or even three babies at a time like people do. They have six, or seven, or eight, or something like that. And one hamster, who lived in Louisiana, in America, had 26 babies at a time, and that hamster got in the book of *Guinness World Records*.

We picked the other phone up again to listen.

The Pet Shop Man said, 'She can't be pregnant because both the hamsters I sold you are female.'

Mum said, 'Maybe it was pregnant before it left the shop.'

The Pet Shop Man said, 'No. Impossible. It was only three weeks old, and every single hamster in this shop is female.'

Mum said, 'Well, what are you suggesting, an immaculate conception?'

I know all about what an immaculate conception is because I was the Angel Gabriel in the Nativity at Church last year, and I had to visit Mary to tell her she was going to have a baby, and when Mary said to me, 'How shall this be, seeing that I know not a man?' I had to say, 'The Holy Ghost shall come upon thee, and the power of the Highest shall overshadow thee: therefore also that holy thing which shall be born of thee shall be called the Son of God. For with God nothing shall be impossible.'

And that's what an immaculate conception is. But it doesn't happen with hamsters because I don't think it ever even happens with people, apart from Mary. Maybe.

Anyway, the Pet Shop Man said, 'Maybe your hamster has just got wind.'

And Mum said, 'It's been getting fatter for weeks.'

And the Pet Shop man said, 'Or it could be a Phantom Pregnancy.'

And I said, 'What's a Phantom Pregnancy?'

And Mum said,

'PUT THE PHONE DOWN!'

And then she said, 'How do I check if the other hamster is male?'

And the Pet Shop Man told her how.

Mum put the phone down. And me and Tom put the other phone down. And we ran back into my room and we sat on the bed.

Mum came in, and she picked Number Two

up, and she turned Number Two on her back to look at her tummy. Number Two didn't like being on her back, and she bit Mum, and then Mum dropped Number Two, and she couldn't catch her for ages, and each time she did catch her, Number Two bit her again.

I got the gardening gloves and I put Number Two back in the fish-tank. Mum said she would look at Number Two again tomorrow when she could take her by surprise.

I asked Mum what a Phantom Pregnancy was again.

Mum said, 'It's nothing, Big Ears. It's time for bed.'

It didn't sound like nothing to me. It didn't have Phantom Pregnancy in the dictionary in my house, but it did have Phantom, and it didn't sound very good.

This is what it said...

phantom [fan-tum] ✦ *noun*
a spirit of a dead person believed by
some to visit the living as a pale, almost
transparent form of a person, animal or
other object; a ghost

I wanted to knock on the wall to ask Suzanne
what it said in the dictionary in her house about
phantoms, in case the ones in my dictionary
weren't the right kind. But I knew Suzanne
wouldn't knock back. So I went to bed instead.

●? ●? ●?

I had a dream. A bad one. About Nanna. She was
in the back lane, and she was see-through, like
a phantom, and she was digging in the ground
trying to find the Old Rabbit. When I woke up it

104

was still dark. I looked at my clock. It was 2.00 a.m. That means it was two o'clock in the morning. I've got a digital clock because I'm not very good with the time.

Anyway, it was the middle of the night, and the hamster wheel was squeaking. I took the lid off the fish-tank. Hamster Number Two was on the wheel. I pulled back some of the tissue paper from the top of the nest to see if Number One was in there. And she was. And next to Number One was a pale pink see-through thing that was moving. And when I looked closer it wasn't *one*

pale pink see-through thing that was moving, it was *lots* of little pale pink see-through things.

They were tiny, like small prawns, and you could see all their veins, and you could even see their hearts beating through their skin. At first I thought they must be phantoms like the Pet Shop Man said, and like it said in the dictionary, but then I looked in the Hamster Manual.

I couldn't really understand what it said about baby hamsters because of it using lots of hard words, but it had a picture of some babies, and they looked exactly like the Phantom Hamsters in the fish-tank. So I decided they probably weren't Phantom Hamsters after all, even though they looked all pale and everything, because that's how they looked in the book too, and anyway when Tom was born he looked a bit pale and see-through too and *he* wasn't a phantom.

I went into Tom's room and woke him up and he came to see.

'Oh, look!' he said, 'There's millions of them.' And he laughed, and then he hopped about from one foot to the other like he does when he needs a wee, but faster. And I did it too because that's the dance that me and Tom do sometimes, when something we love happens.

Tom said, 'Count them. Count them!'

I counted the babies and there were eight. And then me and Tom got The Hysterics a bit, and we had to put our heads under the duvet so we didn't wake Mum up. And we had The Hysterics for ages. Because now we had eight new Baby Hamsters, and soon their eyes would open, and they would stop looking like phantoms, and start growing, and getting fur, and running around. And we would have ten hamsters altogether, and they could all do the obstacle course. And because as soon as we could tell them apart we would have to think of eight names for the new ones. And because we would never have been allowed eight more hamsters if we had asked but now that we had them, no one could take them away because they would have to stay with their mum until they were all grown-up.

I put the lid back on the fish-tank. Or at least I meant to put the lid back on the fish-tank. And I shut my bedroom door. Or at least I meant to shut my bedroom door. And Tom got in my bed, because I didn't feel like sleeping on my own very much. And we talked about the Baby Hamsters, and what we might call them. And then we fell asleep.

And when I woke up it was because Tom said, 'Ugh!'

CHAPTER 14

The Hamster MASSACRE

'Look,' Tom said. He pointed at the fish-tank.

There were spots on the glass. And the sawdust near the nest was wet. I lifted up the tissue paper. It was sticky and red. And underneath, in the middle, were the eight Baby Hamsters. They were covered in blood. And all of them were dead. Number One was in the corner of the tank. She had blood around her mouth, and one of her back legs had gone. And the other thing that had gone was Hamster Number Two.

'There's only one hamster left,' Tom said.

And I said, 'MUUUUUUUUUUM!'

❝ CHAPTER 15 ❞

In Shock

The Vet put three stitches in the end of the stump where Number One's back foot used to be. Number One didn't move, and she didn't even squeak. The Vet said she thought that Number One was in shock. And I said I thought Number One was in shock too, because I would be in shock if something bit my back leg off and killed all my babies and kidnapped my friend.

But The Vet said, 'I'm afraid to say this hamster probably killed the babies herself. It's quite common. You see, the male hamster becomes more and more aggressive during the pregnancy, and the female feels threatened, and eliminates her dependants. You weren't to know, but it's a standard response. I'm very sorry.'

I didn't really know what eliminates or dependants or standard was, but I said that one thing I *did* know was that Number One wouldn't kill her own babies, even if she did feel threatened, because she wasn't really that kind of hamster. And I also knew for another thing that Number Two wasn't a male hamster because the Pet Shop Man had said she was a female.

The Vet said, 'Mmm, the Pet Shop Man. How long have you had the hamsters?'

And I said, 'five weeks.'

And The Vet said, 'Well, there you are, you see. The gestation period of a hamster, which is to say the time from conception to birth, is around twenty-one days.'

I didn't say anything.

The Vet said, 'How old are you?'

I didn't see what how old I was had to do with anything but I said, 'I am nine' anyway, and The Vet said, 'How can I put it? Urm... It's like this. A girl buys two hamsters. She has had the hamsters for five weeks when one of the hamsters gives birth. The length of time for which hamsters are pregnant is around three weeks. Did the hamster become pregnant before or after the girl bought it? And, if the hamster became pregnant *after* the girl bought it, what sex was the other hamster?'

I looked at my trainers because I hate sums

and I hate riddles, and I especially hate it when someone is staring at you and waiting for you to answer because it stops you being able to think, so I undid the laces on my trainers. And then I did them back up again.

And Mum said, 'You see? Unless it *was* an immaculate conception.'

I said, 'No. It wasn't an immaculate conception because hamsters don't have immaculate conceptions because that only happened to Mary.'

And then The Vet laughed. Even though it wasn't funny and even though vets aren't supposed to ask people sums or riddles or laugh at jokes or anything like that because they're supposed to just look at the pets and do the stitches.

I said, 'Even if Number Two *was* a male that

114

doesn't mean it was him who bit Number One's leg off, because it could have been something else. Because anyone could have got in the fish-tank and taken Number Two away and bitten Number One's leg off and killed the babies.'

And Mum said, 'Like who?'

And I said, 'Like the New Cat.'

And The Vet said, 'This wound is not consistent with something that might be inflicted by a cat, I'm afraid. Also, a cat would not leave Hamster Number One alive, and it would not cover the Baby Hamsters over, and leave them dead in the nest. Cats take their kills away with them, you see.'

I didn't say anything because The Vet didn't know what the New Cat was like. Because the New Cat didn't just bite things, sometimes she killed things by scaring them to death and things like that. Like with the Old Rabbit. And foxes sometimes kill chickens and just leave them. Graham Roberts told me that, and his Dad is a farmer, and they know more about things killing things than vets do.

I said, 'Well, where is Number Two now?'

And The Vet said, 'That is the question. It must have escaped.'

But I didn't think that Number Two had escaped because, even though I might have forgotten to put the lid on the fish-tank, and even though I might have left my bedroom door open, Number Two couldn't climb up the glass. Not unless it got on top of the wheel. And Number Two had only ever got on top of the wheel once before because it was a very hard thing to do.

Anyway, I didn't speak to The Vet after that because she said that she didn't think that Number One would live very long without her leg. And I wanted to go home.

When we got back to the house I went upstairs to have a look at the dead Baby Hamsters. But the dead Baby Hamsters weren't there because Dad had cleaned the fish-tank out, and he had put new sawdust in, and he had made it look like nothing had ever even happened. Just like in Nanna's room. And he had got all the old sawdust, and the nest with the blood, and all the Baby Hamsters, and put them in a carrier bag. And he had put the carrier bag in the outside bin.

I ran out the back. Dad shouted after me, and Mum grabbed me by my hood, but I wriggled out of my coat, and I got away, and I got the carrier bag out of the bin, and Dad said, 'Put it back.'

And I said,

'THEY DON'T GO IN THE BIN!'

And I ran past Mum and Dad and upstairs to my room, and I shut the door, and sat against it. And Mum and Dad and Tom wanted to come in but I didn't let them because Dad had put the hamsters in the bin, and Mum didn't even want the hamsters in the first place, and Tom said 'Ugh' about the babies.

And I sat against the door until they all went away. And then I looked inside the carrier bag. I took out the nest, and I picked the eight Baby Hamsters out, one by one, and they were cold, and wet, and I put them on some tissue in my sandwich box. And then I put the lid on the box. And then I cried. And I couldn't stop crying. And I didn't want to.

After ages I heard three knocks on the wall. I stopped crying and I went to my window and I opened it. Suzanne opened her window too. She got out on the window ledge. 'I heard about your hamsters,' she said.

I said, 'Number Two has gone missing and Number One has only got three legs left and she had to have stitches and she had eight babies and they're all dead and Dad put them in the bin and I got them out.'

Suzanne said 'Can I see?'

So I lifted up the lid on the sandwich box and showed her the eight tiny hamsters in a row on the tissue.

Suzanne said, 'They don't look like hamsters.'

Because they didn't really.

I said, 'It's because they are a bit mushed and they haven't got their fur yet.' And then I put the lid back on the hamsters and I started crying again because they never would get any fur because they were dead, and because they were so small, and because they hadn't even opened their eyes yet, and because Dad put them in the bin, and because I didn't want Number Two to have bitten Number One's leg off and escaped, and because I didn't want Number One to have killed all the babies.

But Suzanne said, 'Maybe it wasn't Number Two who bit Number One's leg off, and maybe it wasn't Number One who killed the babies because maybe it was someone else, and maybe you are right about the New Cat, or the fox, and maybe we could find out what really happened and who really killed the hamsters because we could do an investigation!'

And then Suzanne said she would help me to do an investigation. And she would help me to bury the Baby Hamsters too, if I liked.

I said, 'I haven't got anything little enough to bury them in.'

But Suzanne said that she did. And she said she would bring all the things that we needed for burying the hamsters over to the shed.

And then she said, 'You can choose the password.'

I said, 'The password should be Dead.'

And Suzanne said, 'Yes.'

CHAPTER 16
Ashes To Ashes

Suzanne brought eight matchboxes. And she brought coloured paper. And all her pens. And glue. And glitter. And her best shells from the beach to stick on the boxes. And she brought some twigs and some twine to make crosses. And a shoebox that she had covered in black paper with red ribbon to put around it.

'It's for the Old Rabbit,' she said. Because if I didn't mind, she said, we could dig the Old Rabbit up and bury it again at the same time as the hamsters. And I didn't mind. So that is what we decided to do.

We stayed in the shed making the boxes for the Baby Hamsters all day, and we did them in eight different colours, and Mum brought us some sandwiches, and we didn't even come out for lunch, and we stuck a shell on each one, and some glitter, and we put a little bit of grass in them to make it nice inside.

When they were all done, I opened the lid of the sandwich box with the dead Baby Hamsters in, and I took the Baby Hamsters out one at a time, and I picked the sawdust off them, and the tissue paper, and Suzanne wiped the blood with her hankie. And I put each one in its own box. And I made eight holes in the ground next to where the Old Cat was buried, and Suzanne put the eight little stick crosses in the ground behind the holes. And then we went and got Tom, and then me and Suzanne and Tom went and got Joe-down-the-road.

The crisp packet that Joe had put under a stone to show where the Old Rabbit was buried wasn't there anymore. But Joe said he knew exactly where it was anyway, and he pointed to the spot.

I started to dig. I didn't dig with the trowel like I did for the eight hamster holes because Joe said I might dig through the Old Rabbit.

So I dug with my hands, and after a while I could feel something hard. I flicked all the mud off the hard thing, and I could feel that the hard thing had fur on. The Old Rabbit looked very old in the ground. And it smelled.

Joe said he hoped there weren't any worms, and there weren't, but there were some maggots because some of them fell out of the Old Rabbit's mouth when I got it out of the ground. But Joe didn't see, and I brushed the mud away from the Old Rabbit's face, and out of its eyes before I showed it to him. And I showed him the side with the closed eye because on the other side the eye was still open, and it had gone a bit funny, and I didn't think Joe would like it.

Joe stroked the Old Rabbit on its nose, and he wiped its body with Suzanne's hankie, and made its fur all smooth, and then he held the Old Rabbit to his cheek, and after that he put the Old Rabbit in the box, on the straw, and Suzanne put a dandelion in, and I put the lid on, and I put the box in the ground, and I covered it over, and Suzanne put a cross in the ground behind it.

And then Joe said he had to go because even though he liked the Old Rabbit best, the New Cat might be hunting the New Rabbit for all he knew, and he had to go back to sit on the hutch with his Super Soaker, just in case.

Suzanne put the eight Baby Hamsters in the ground and I covered them over. Suzanne said we should all say something about the Baby Hamsters. I didn't want to say anything about them because I couldn't really think of anything except that they looked a bit like prawns, and I didn't want to say that. But Suzanne said it wasn't really a proper funeral if no one said anything.

So Suzanne said, 'They didn't look like hamsters but they were. They just hadn't got their fur yet.'

Which was true.

And I said, 'They were born in the night and in the morning they were dead.'

Which was also true.

And Tom said, 'They are under the mud.'

Which was true as well. And which was better than at Nanna's funeral because there the Vicar kept saying how Nanna never had a bad word to say about anyone. And that wasn't true because Nanna did have a bad word to say about some people sometimes. Like Suzanne's Dad, and Miss Matheson, and Joe-down-the-road's Mum's Boyfriend. But she never said a bad word about me, or Tom, or Vera off 'Coronation Street'.

CHAPTER 17
A Real Investigation

In the morning, when Suzanne knocked on the wall three times, me and Tom were ready. We met at the shed at eight o'clock and Suzanne said we should call it 'Oh, Eight Hundred Hours', so we did. Suzanne's Mum watches all the police dramas on telly, and Suzanne does too, even the late ones that I'm not allowed to watch, and that's how Suzanne knows all about exactly what you should call things in a Real Investigation.

Suzanne said the first thing we should do was have a meeting. The password was Investigation. Tom didn't like the password being Investigation at first because it's quite a hard word, because he's only five, and he kept calling it 'In-ges-tiv-ation'.

I said it didn't matter if Tom got the password a little bit wrong, as long as it was nearly right.

And Suzanne said it didn't really even matter if he couldn't remember it at all, because he could just say, 'Hello, it's me, Tom' like he always does, because he always ends up forgetting what the password is anyway.

After we had the meeting and decided on the password, I said I thought we should go and see Mrs Rotherham up the road because she would know what to do because she used to be in the police.

Tom didn't want to go because he is scared of Mrs Rotherham. He thought we should go in the house and see Mum and have a biscuit instead. But Suzanne said that having a biscuit definitely wasn't the next thing to do.

I'm not scared of Mrs Rotherham. I wasn't that scared of her in the first place but I'm really not scared of her now because at Nanna's funeral, Mrs Rotherham gave me her hankie and, after I'd blown my nose on it, she said I could keep it. It's a really old hankie, probably about a hundred years old or something, and it's got lace on. Mrs Rotherham made it herself.

Anyway, Mum hadn't told Mrs Rotherham any of the bad things about me and Tom that she always said she had half a mind to. Or, if she had, Mrs Rotherham didn't seem to care. Mrs Rotherham winked at me when the Vicar was saying how Nanna never said a bad word about anyone. And afterwards she showed me how to wink. I can only do it with one eye. I'm practising with the other one. Mrs Rotherham said I could come to her house whenever I liked.

Tom said he would come up the road with me and Suzanne as long as he could wait outside. So that is what we did.

●: ●: ●:

Mrs Rotherham's house smells of old things, and mothballs, the same as Nanna's used to. Most old ladies' houses smell a bit the same when they are really old. It's a funny smell, a bit like the old cupboard upstairs at Sunday School. Our house will probably smell like that soon because Mum keeps finding grey hairs on her head and that means she must be nearly old too.

Anyway, I told Mrs Rotherham all about what happened to the hamsters. Mrs Rotherham said, 'Well, well, well.' And then she said 'Oh dear, oh dear, oh dear.' Which Suzanne said afterwards is what police people used to say in the olden days. And then she said, 'A *massacre!*'

I told Mrs Rotherham all about what The Vet had said about how she thought that Number Two had bitten Number One's leg off, and how she thought Number One had killed all the babies, and how she thought Number Two had escaped.

Mrs Rotherham said, 'The Vet is probably right.'

And I said 'Oh,' because for one thing that wasn't really what I wanted Mrs Rotherham to say, and for another thing it didn't really help us with our investigation.

Suzanne told Mrs Rotherham how we were

doing an investigation, and how we thought Mrs Rotherham might be able to help because, she said, 'Maybe The Vet *wasn't* right, and maybe someone else killed the hamsters, and maybe seeing as how you used to be in the Police, you could help us catch whoever it was by telling us what to do in a Real Investigation.'

Mrs Rotherham said, 'I see. The Vet probably is right. But, in a Real Investigation, probably is not good enough. *Probably* doesn't come into it.'

And then she winked.

'The first thing to do in a Real Investigation – particularly a murder investigation – and particularly a mass-murder investigation, such as this one, is to get yourself a nice cup of tea, and a biscuit.'

And she went into the kitchen. After a while she

came back with the tea, and with some biscuits, and she poured the tea out, and she put the milk in, and the sugars, because she said sweet tea was best for this sort of thing. And she drank her tea, and we drank our tea.

And then she said, 'Is your brother going to come in?'

I said he wasn't.

Mrs Rotherham said, 'Only it's raining.'

And I said, 'Tom doesn't mind if it's raining.'

Which he didn't.

'Because,' I said, 'once me and Tom went out and stood in the rain for ages on purpose to see how wet we could get and we got really, really wet and that was about the best thing Tom said he had ever done...'

Suzanne said we didn't have time to talk about

Tom and the rain, and we had to get on with the investigation.

Mrs Rotherham said, 'Quite right.' And she looked very serious. And then she said, 'You will need these.' And she gave us a small notepad and a pencil. And then she said, 'And you might need this.' And she gave us a magnifying glass. And then she said, 'And this.' And she gave us a Dictaphone, which is a thing for recording what people say, and it's got a little tape inside. And then she said, 'And you will definitely need this', and she gave us a real police badge. And then Mrs Rotherham wrote on a piece of paper for quite a long time. And she put the piece of paper in an envelope. And she wrote 'Investigation Instructions' on the envelope and she gave the envelope to Suzanne. And she gave me three biscuits to give to Tom.

And then she said, 'I'll expect you back before tea-time.'

Tom was still waiting outside, and he was quite wet, especially his feet because he was waiting in a puddle. But he didn't mind, and he was very pleased about the biscuits, especially when we told him that Mrs Rotherham said that tea and biscuits were the first things that you should do in a Real Investigation. Because Tom said he thought that they might be.

And then me and Suzanne and Tom went back
to the shed.

❝ CHAPTER 18 ❞
Who Done It?

Suzanne opened the envelope and she read out what it said on the piece of paper. And then I read out what it said on the piece of paper again because Suzanne isn't all that good at reading sometimes, and Mrs Rotherham's handwriting was quite curly like Nanna's used to be, like old people always write, and it was quite shaky too, and Suzanne kept getting the words wrong.

The first thing it said on Mrs Rotherham's piece of paper was…

MAKE A LIST OF SUSPECTS
To do this you will need...

a) Your notepad and pencil

b) Your brain

You must ask yourself the following questions:

1. Who do you think might have murdered the hamsters?

2. Have they done or said anything that makes you suspect them?

3. Do they have any prior record of violence or murder? (This means have they done something like it before)

(Tip: A hunch is as good a reason as any to make someone a suspect.)

We thought of some suspects and I wrote them down. We had eight suspects altogether. We did have nine but then Suzanne said she thought we should take one of them off, which was the Fox, because she said, 'No one has seen a fox in the street, and a fox would be too big to get in through the cat flap, and it wouldn't be able to get in the house any other way.'

I said, 'I think a fox might be able to get through the cat flap, if it was a very skinny one.'

But Tom said, 'I am smaller than a fox, and *I* can't get through the cat flap because I have tried lots of times and I always get stuck.'

So this is what it said on our suspects list…

ANNA'S AND SUZANNE'S AND TOM'S LIST OF SUSPECTS FOR THE HAMSTER MASSACRE INVESTIGATION

1. Mr Tucker

Because...

a) He doesn't like Russians

b) He called the hamsters "Gremlins"

2. Joe-down-the-road's Mum's Boyfriend

Because...

a) We have got a hunch

b)?

3. Hamster Number Two

Because...

a) He used to bite a lot and he could have bitten Number One's leg off and killed the babies and escaped

4. The New Cat

Because...

a) She is always crouching near my bedroom door in a hunting kind of way

b) She has already killed four Sparrows, three Field Mice, five Moths, eight Spiders, one Bumble Bee and scared the Old Rabbit to death

5. Mum

Because...

a) She didn't want the hamsters in the first place

b) She has already killed two hamsters called Geoff and Bernard

6. Suzanne's Dad

Because...

a) He 'HATES PETS'

7. Hamster Number One

Because...

a) She was in the cage at the time

b) The Vet said so

c) Mum said so

d) Dad said so

e) The internet said so

f) The chapter called 'Severely Stressed Hamsters' in the *Hamsters – A Manual* book said so.

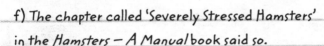

8. Miss Matheson

Because...

a) She killed the Old Cat

b) She doesn't like people on her private property

The next thing it said to do on Mrs Rotherham's piece of paper after making a list of suspects was…

INTERVIEW YOUR SUSPECTS

To do this you will need…

1) Your police badge

2) Your notepad and pencil

3) Your Dictaphone to record the interviews

4) Your magnifying glass to look for clues

146

You should...

1. Ask the suspects where they were when the massacre was committed.

2. Ask them to prove that they were where they say they were (Do they have an alibi? Was someone with them at the time?)

3. If they have a solid alibi you must eliminate them from your investigation (cross them off the suspect list).

This is what it says an alibi is in my dictionary...

alibi [al-uh-by] ♦ *noun*
proof that someone who is thought to have committed a crime could not have done it, especially the fact or claim that they were in another place at the time it happened.

We didn't check what it said in the dictionary in Suzanne's house because for one thing the dictionary in Suzanne's house always ends up getting us into trouble, and for another thing my dictionary sounded like it had the right kind of alibi in it. We decided I would be the one to tell people what had happened with the hamsters, and to press record on the Dictaphone when people started talking, because I was the only one with pockets big enough to fit the Dictaphone in, and if people knew they were being recorded they might not like it. And Suzanne would be the one to hold the real police badge and ask the questions and write in the notepad. And Tom would be the one to hold the magnifying glass and look for clues.

The first suspect on our list was Mr Tucker.

I didn't really want to go to Mr Tucker's house first because I thought we might get stuck talking about litter and everything, but Tom said he wanted to see Mr Tucker anyway and Suzanne said that she would hold up the police badge and tell Mr Tucker that we didn't have time to talk about litter.

So we went and knocked on Mr Tucker's door.

● ● ●

I told Mr Tucker how the eight Baby Hamsters were dead and how Number Two was missing and how Number One only had three legs left.

Mr Tucker said, 'Good God! A wilding! You had better come in. If you ask me—'

But Suzanne got the police badge out.

And she said, 'Mr Tucker. Where were your whereabouts between the hours of two a.m. and seven a.m. on Thursday morning?'

Mr Tucker said, 'So, that's how it is, eh?'

And he sat down and said, 'In bed. Civvy kip. Where else should an old lag be?'

Tom put the magnifying glass up close to Mr Tucker's face and looked him up and down. Mr Tucker's eye bulged through the glass.

Mr Tucker said, 'A snoop! Tom! I didn't have you down for that, Old Chum.'

Suzanne said, 'Was anyone else in bed with you?'

And Mr Tucker said, 'Mrs Tucker, of course. Upstart!'

And then he shouted up the stairs, **'DICKEY. COME DOWN, WILL YOU!'**

And Mrs Tucker came down.

Mr Tucker said, 'Now, Dickey, don't fold up. Give 'em a good show, and for God's sake keep doggo about the bodies out the back.' And then he pulled faces at Tom through the magnifying glass.

Suzanne said, 'Name?' to Mrs Tucker.

And Mrs Tucker said, 'Dickey Tucker.'

And then we had to stop for a bit because Suzanne had to go the toilet.

When Suzanne came back from the toilet, Mrs Tucker said that Mr Tucker was definitely in bed asleep between two a.m. and seven a.m. on Thursday, because she was there too, and she is a very light sleeper, and she said, 'Mr Tucker snores a lot, and thrashes about, and shouts out, and I was wide awake reading. I haven't slept more than four hours a night since 1945.'

I was not sure Mrs Tucker was telling the truth but she took her glasses off and pointed to the bags under her eyes, and Tom looked at them with the magnifying glass, and they were very big. And then Mr Tucker pretended to fall asleep in the chair and he did lots of snoring and he shouted, 'We're hit. We're hit. One engine down. Come in, Charlie!'

And Tom thought that was the best thing ever and he laughed a lot.

And then Mr Tucker picked Tom up, and flew him round the room.

And then he sat down because Mrs Tucker said, 'Stop it, Raymond! You'll give yourself a heart attack.'

And then she went to get some lemonade.

We drank the lemonade and said, 'thank you' to Mrs Tucker. And then we crossed Mr Tucker off the Suspect List.

The next person on our list was Joe-down-the-road's Mum's Boyfriend. Because we had a hunch about him. And Mrs Rotherham had said that a hunch was as good a reason as any.

Joe was sitting on the New Rabbit's hutch in the backyard with the Super Soaker. We asked Joe if his Mum's Boyfriend was there. But Joe didn't answer. Joe never answers if he doesn't want to.

153

Joe's Mum was standing looking out of the back window.

I told Joe's Mum about what had happened with the hamsters and how we were asking people if they had seen anything unusual and Suzanne said, 'Can you tell us where your boyfriend's whereabouts were between two a.m. and seven a.m. on Thursday?'

And Joe's Mum said, 'I can tell you *exactly* where his whereabouts were between two a.m. and seven a.m. on Thursday. His whereabouts were in Kuala bloomin' Lumpur. In the Mandarin Oriental Hotel. And the babysitter's whereabouts were there as well!'

And she showed us Kuala Lumpur on Joe's globe. It's a long way away.

KUALA
LUMPUR

And then she showed us her Boyfriend's bank statement. And Tom looked at it through the magnifying glass. It said,

£ BANK STATEMENT

Date	payment type and details	paid out
30 Aug	DELUXE SUITE, MANDARIN ORIENTAL, KUALA LUMPUR	£268.50

We said thank you to Joe's Mum, and she gave Tom a biscuit, because he asked for one. And we crossed her Boyfriend off the list.

●: ●: ●:

The next suspect on the list was Hamster Number Two. We couldn't interview Number Two because

155

he was still missing. And even though we had put trails of food out every night, he hadn't come back yet.

So Suzanne wrote 'missing' next to Number Two's name on the Suspect List. And we went to find the New Cat.

●⁊ ●⁊ ●⁊

It was a bit difficult to interview the New Cat because of her being a cat, and because she couldn't answer the questions, but Tom said he just wanted to look the New Cat in the eye with the magnifying glass to see if he could tell anything by that.

The New Cat looked even angrier than ever through the magnifying glass. She hissed at Tom and made her fur go big. And then Tom tried to pick the New Cat up. And the New Cat bit Tom really hard. And then Tom bit the New Cat back, even harder. And the New Cat looked very surprised because no one had ever bitten her back before. And Tom looked quite surprised too because he had never bitten a cat before either. And also because he had quite a lot of the New Cat's fur in his mouth.

Tom said he wanted to go and see Mum to get the fur out of his mouth. And Mum was the next person on our list anyway. So that is what we did.

●} ●} ●}

Mum didn't really like being questioned. She made Tom put the magnifying glass down, and she made Suzanne put the notepad down. But she didn't make me turn the Dictaphone off because she didn't know it was on record in my pocket.

Mum said, 'We've been through all this already. You know fine well that I was in bed. And that I didn't hear anything. This is getting beyond a joke.'

I said 'It never was a joke,' because it wasn't.

I said, 'It's an investigation.'

But Mum said, 'It's not healthy. All this digging about death. And you shouldn't be dragging poor Suzanne into it.'

Suzanne said how she wasn't being dragged into it because she was in charge, actually.

But Mum said, 'The *investigation* is *over*. If you don't drop it, right now, and accept that Number One killed the babies, and Number Two bit her leg off and escaped, then I am sending Suzanne home. And I'm going to phone Mrs Rotherham because I'm cross that she is encouraging all of this.'

So we promised that we would drop it, and that we wouldn't investigate anyone else, and we crossed Mum off the list.

And we just went to investigate Suzanne's Dad and Number One and Miss Matheson very quickly because they were the only suspects left.

When we got to Suzanne's house, Suzanne's Dad was in the bathroom. Suzanne banged on the door.

Suzanne's Dad shouted, **'I'M ON THE TOILET, FOR CRYING OUT LOUD!'**

Suzanne said that her Dad sometimes sits on the toilet for hours. We didn't have time to wait for him to get off the toilet, especially because

Suzanne said she didn't think her Dad was in a very good mood anyway, not enough to be asked about his whereabouts, so we asked Suzanne's Mum instead.

I told Suzanne's Mum all about what had happened with the hamsters and everything.

Suzanne's Mum said My Mum had already told her.

Suzanne said, 'Yes, but can you tell us about where Dad's whereabouts were between two a.m. and seven a.m. on Thursday morning?'

Suzanne's Mum said, 'Yes. He was here. Up and down with his piles all night.'

I said, 'What are piles?'

Suzanne's Mum said, 'I haven't got time to stand around talking about piles all day. You get them in your bottom. They aren't very nice.'

160

This is what it says about piles in the dictionary in Suzanne's house…

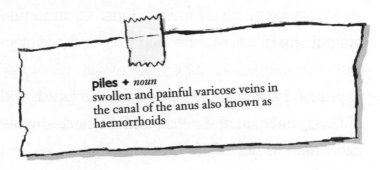

piles ✦ *noun*
swollen and painful varicose veins in the canal of the anus also known as haemorrhoids

We crossed Suzanne's Dad off the list and we went to see Hamster Number One.

Number One was in the nest. I peeled back the top of the nest and picked Number One up and stroked her on the head. I could feel the stitches where her leg used to be. Number One looked very thin, and her fur was all matted, and she didn't even open her eyes.

I said, 'I think Number One is too sick to be interviewed.'

Tom looked at Number One through the magnifying glass. And he said that he thought so too.

I gave Number One a kiss on the head, and put her back in the nest, and Suzanne wrote 'Sick' next to her name on the Suspect List, and said we should come back when Number One was better.

And then we went to see Miss Matheson.

Miss Matheson didn't take the chain off when she answered the door. I told her what had happened to the hamsters through the crack.

Suzanne showed Miss Matheson the real police badge and said, 'We need to know where your whereabouts were between two a.m. and seven a.m. on Thursday, Miss Matheson.'

Miss Matheson took the chain off the door and said, **'GET OFF MY PROPERTY BEFORE I CALL THE POLICE! I WARNED YOU ABOUT ALL THIS LAST TIME WITH THAT AWFUL OLD CAT. THIS IS TRESPASS. I'VE KEPT A RECORD!'**

So we ran up the road to Mrs Rotherham's because we were already late and because it was seventeen hundred and a half hours and that is after tea-time.

And Tom said he would come into Mrs Rotherham's house with us because he wasn't scared of her anymore and because he liked her biscuits.

CHAPTER 19
The Hysterics

Mrs Rotherham loved it when we played her all the interviews on the Dictaphone. She said it was the best thing she had ever heard in her life. Mrs Rotherham got The Hysterics.

Me and Tom and Suzanne got The Hysterics a bit too, but not as much as Mrs Rotherham.

Mrs Rotherham got The Hysterics all the way through. She got them so badly she had to lie on the floor. She said it was a shame that Nanna wasn't there because Nanna would have got The Hysterics as well. And she would. Because it was almost as funny as when Graham Roberts was Jesus, just in his pants.

Tom said, 'Nanna said ice cream is good when you need to calm down.'

And Mrs Rotherham went and got some out of the freezer.

After we ate the ice cream, and Mrs Rotherham calmed down, Suzanne showed Mrs Rotherham the Suspect List.

Mrs Rotherham said, 'So, Mr Tucker, Joe-down-the-road's Mum's Boyfriend, Your Mum, and Suzanne's Dad all have solid alibis and are eliminated from the investigation, which means that it had to be either Hamster Number One, or Hamster Number Two, or The New Cat, or Miss Matheson who committed the massacre.'

Mrs Rotherham's phone rang.

Mrs Rotherham answered the phone and said, 'Hello.' And then she said, 'It's your Mum.' And then she winked.

And then she spoke into the phone and said, 'Ah. I see. Leave it with me. Goodbye.'

Mrs Rotherham put the phone down. She looked very serious.

And she said, 'I must inform you that

the Investigation into the Hamster Massacre, although unsolved, is now, and until further notice, officially closed.'

I said, 'Why?'

Mrs Rotherham said, 'The usual reasons: lack of funding, and manpower, and evidence, and missing and uncooperative suspects and witnesses. And because it's unlikely that new evidence will come to light at this late stage. Those are the main reasons.

'And also because Miss Matheson has called Your Mum to complain, and also because your tea is ready.'

Tom said, 'Let's go home', because he didn't want to do an investigation anymore because he was hungry, and he needed a wee, and because, he said, 'It's probably Miss Matheson that did the murder anyway. It was her the last time.'

I said, 'Suzanne found cat blood on her tyres.'

And Mrs Rotherham said, 'Well done.'

Suzanne said, 'It was red.'

Tom said, 'Have you got any biscuits?'

Mrs Rotherham said she did. And she gave Tom a biscuit, and Tom gave her back the magnifying glass, and I gave her the Dictaphone, and Suzanne gave her the police badge but Mrs Rotherham said we could keep the notebook. And she said we should come back whenever we wanted, and especially if there was ever another investigation.

And Suzanne said, 'There probably will be.'

Because there quite often is.

And we went back to the shed and we put the investigation notebook next to the worm box and the wasp trap and the pictures that we traced from Joe-down-the-road's Mum's book.

˙˚ CHAPTER 20 ˚˙
What I Did In My Summer Holidays

So that's pretty much everything that has happened with the hamsters and everything. Except that Number One died in the night. It was three days after Mrs Rotherham closed the Real Investigation.

We didn't really do a funeral for Number One because for one thing Tom said he was sick of doing funerals, and for another thing I couldn't think of anything to say. Suzanne says if you don't say something it isn't really a funeral at all, which is true.

I buried Number One on my own. I dug a hole next to the eight Baby Hamsters and I put her in

there. I put her in a box but I didn't
decorate it. And I
didn't put a cross
in the ground
either.

Mum said I could get another hamster if I
wanted to. Just one. On its own. But I don't really
want to. Tom says he doesn't want to either
because he said the New Cat wouldn't like it.
I don't really care about the New Cat but ever
since Tom bit the New Cat back, Tom does.

That's when the New Cat started following Tom
around. The New Cat follows Tom everywhere
now, even when he's busy holding the bin bag
for Mr Tucker, or walking in a straight line with
his eyes closed, or collecting gravel, the New
Cat goes too. I don't think I would like it if the

New Cat followed *me* around. But Tom does. Sometimes the New Cat sleeps on Tom's bed. And sometimes it puts dead things on his pillow.

I won't sleep in Tom's bed anymore because for one thing I don't like it that the New Cat might put a dead thing in it, and for another thing I'm too old to sleep in Tom's bed really, because I'm nine, and for an even other thing it's school again tomorrow. And you have to sleep in your own bed when it's school again.

I really am supposed to be doing my What-I-Did-In-My-Summer-Holidays Story for school now. I still can't remember any nice things to put in it. But, like Mum says, I can just make some nice things up because it's only a holiday story. So it doesn't really matter if it's not exactly true. Not like when you're writing up a Real Investigation. You can't make anything up at all when you're writing one of those. With a Real Investigation you have to write everything exactly right. And you have to write it straight away. That's what Suzanne says. And that's what I did.

The End

THE GREAT
RABBIT
Rescue

Katie Davies

Illustrated by Hannah Shaw

SIMON AND SCHUSTER

For Sam

Thanks to my Mum and Dad, and to my husband, Alan, for reading (and reading) it.

And thanks also to my agent, Clare Conville, and to Venetia Gosling and everyone at Simon and Schuster.

CHAPTER 1
A Real Rescue

This is a story about Joe-down-the-road, and why he went away, and how he got rescued. Most stories I've read about people getting rescued aren't *Real-Life* Stories. They're Fairy Stories, about Sleeping Beauty, and Rapunzel, and people like that. And they probably aren't true because, in Real Life, people don't prick their fingers on spindles very much and fall asleep for a hundred years. And if they did, they probably wouldn't wake up just because someone gave them a kiss on the cheek, like Sleeping Beauty did. Even if the person who kissed them was a Prince.

Because, in Real Life, when people are

really *deep* asleep, you have to shake them, and shout, **'WAKE UP!'** in their ear, and hit them on the head with the xylophone sticks. Otherwise they don't wake up at all.

Fairy Tale
↓

Real Life
↓

My Dad doesn't, anyway. And nor does my little brother, Tom. He falls asleep on the floor, and he doesn't wake up when Mum carries him upstairs and puts him in his pyjamas and stands him up at the toilet. Not even once when he weed on his feet.

Tom is five. He's four years younger than me. I'm nine. My name is Anna.

Also, in Real Life, people don't let down their hair from towers for other people to climb up and rescue them and things, like happens in *Rapunzel*. Because you can't really climb up *hair* very well, especially not when it's still growing on someone's head. You can't climb up Emma Hendry's hair, anyway, because Graham Roberts once tried to, in PE, when Emma was up the wall bars. And Emma fell off, and Mrs Peters wasn't pleased. And neither was Emma. She was winded. Emma's got the longest hair in school. She can sit on it if she wants to. It's never been cut. Mrs Peters sent a note home to Emma's Mum because Emma's hair kept getting caught in doors, and drawers, and things

179

like that, and she said, 'Emma Hendry, that hair is a Death Trap!'

Which is true. Especially with Graham Roberts around. So now Emma's hair gets tied up, and on PE days it has to go under a net.

Anyway, this story isn't a Made-Up Story, or a Fairy Story like *Sleeping Beauty* or *Rapunzel* or anything like that. It's a Real Rescue Story. And that means that everything in it Actually Happened. I know it did because I was there. And so was my little brother, Tom. And so was my friend Suzanne Barry, who lives next door.

This is what it says in my dictionary about what a rescue is…

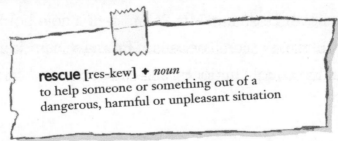

rescue [res-kew] ✦ *noun*
to help someone or something out of a dangerous, harmful or unpleasant situation

And this is what it says in my friend Suzanne's dictionary…

rescue [res-kew] ✦ *informal*
to free or deliver from confinement or peril

Mum said that me and Suzanne and Tom were wrong about Joe-down-the-road and that he was never even *in* any danger or peril in the first place.

She said, 'Anna, Joe has gone to live with his Dad because he *wants* to. He definitely does *not* need to be rescued!'

But mums don't always know everything about who might need rescuing. Because once, when I was in Big Trouble for falling through the shed roof in the back lane by mistake, I decided that I didn't like living at our house anymore, and I told Mum, 'I wish I lived with Mrs Rotherham up the road!'

And Mum said, 'So do I!'

So I packed my bag, and I went off up the road.

When I got to Mrs Rotherham's house, I decided I didn't *really* want to live there. But I had to by then, because that's what I'd said. So I went in. And I sat in the window by myself and stared out and didn't speak. And, after ages, there was a knock on the door. It was Tom, in his Batman pyjamas, and his Bob the Builder hard hat.

And Mrs Rotherham said, 'Hello, Tom, are you all on your own?'

And Tom said, 'I am Batman and Bob the Builder. I want Anna to come home.'

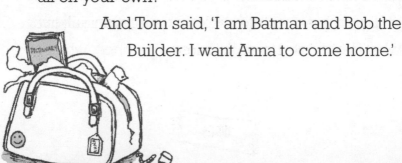

So I did. And that was a rescue, really. What Tom did. Because, even though I like Mrs Rotherham a lot, I didn't *really* want to live with her. Because I'd rather live in my own house, with Tom. And Mum and Dad. And Andy and Joanne (that's my other brother and my sister. They aren't in this story because they're older than me and Tom and they don't really care about rabbits, or rescues). Anyway, if Tom *hadn't* rescued me, I would probably still be living with Mrs Rotherham now. So I'm glad he did. Because, for one thing, Mrs Rotherham's house is at the wrong end of the road. And, for another thing, it smells a bit strange, of old things, and mothballs, like Nanna's house used to. And, for an even other thing, if I lived with Mrs Rotherham I wouldn't live next door to Suzanne anymore.

CHAPTER 2
Anna To Suzanne

Me and Suzanne who lives next door have got walkie-talkies. I talk to Suzanne on my walkie-talkie in my house. And she talks to me on her walkie-talkie in her house.

I hold down the button on the side and say, 'Anna to Suzanne. Anna to Suzanne. Come in, Suzanne. Over.'

And then I let go of the button, and the walkie-talkie crackles, and Suzanne says, 'Suzanne to Anna. Suzanne to Anna. Receiving you loud and clear. Over.'

And that's the way you're supposed to say things when you're on the walkie-talkies. Because Suzanne knows all about it off her uncle in the army. Me and Suzanne talk on our walkie-talkies all the time, wherever we are (except in the bath, because Mum says if it falls in I'll get electrocuted to death like Ken Barlow's first wife on 'Coronation Street').

Mum says she doesn't see why me and Suzanne need walkie-talkies in our houses at all, because the wall between our house and the Barrys' house is so thin we could just put a glass to the wall and talk to each other through that.

Which is true. But putting a glass to the wall isn't as good as talking on walkie-talkies because me and Suzanne tried it.

For one thing, you both have to be in the exact same place on each side of the wall. And for another thing, you can't say anything secret because you have to say everything loud and clear or the other person can't hear it.

And, for an even other thing, if you've got squishy wallpaper on your walls, like Suzanne has in her house, the glass presses a circle shape in the wallpaper. And when Suzanne's Dad sees that, he says, **'GET HERE, SUZANNE! WHAT ON *EARTH* ARE THESE CIRCLE SHAPES ALL OVER THE PLACE?'**

You don't need a glass, or a walkie-talkie, or *anything* to hear Suzanne's *Dad* through the wall. You can hear everything he says, because Suzanne's Dad always shouts.

Before me and Suzanne got the walkie-talkies, we used to have a thing called the Knocking Code. This is how it worked:

I would knock three times on my bedroom wall and, if the coast was clear, Suzanne would knock back three times on her bedroom wall. And then we would both go to our windows, and open them, and crawl out, and sit outside on our window ledges, and talk about things. Like the road, and the roofs, and whether or not you go blind if you stare straight at the sun.

The only thing with the Knocking Code was, sometimes, if there were other noises going on, Suzanne couldn't hear my knocks. And then I had to crawl out onto my window ledge, and over to Suzanne's, to look in through her window, to see if I could see her. And one time when I did that, when Suzanne wasn't there, my window closed behind me. By itself. And I couldn't get it open again. I banged on my window. And nobody came. And I banged on Suzanne's window. And nobody came. And it started raining. And I sat on the window ledge. And I got very wet. And I shouted, **'HELLO!'** and, **'HELP!'** and, **'I'M ON THE WINDOW LEDGE!'**. And after a while I wondered what would be worse, staying on the window ledge and catching my death of cold, like Nanna always used to say I would, or jumping off the window ledge and breaking both my legs.

And just when I was wondering that, Mr Tucker, who lives opposite, came out of his house to put his bins out.

So I shouted down, **'HELP! MR TUCKER! UP HERE! I'M ON THE WINDOW LEDGE!'**

188

Mr Tucker's got a lot of medals from the war. For flying planes, and fighting, and blowing things up and all that. He doesn't fly planes anymore though. He's too old. Most of the time what Mr Tucker does is go up and down the road picking up litter. Nanna used to say Mr Tucker was 'waging a one-man war against rubbish.'

Mr Tucker put his bin bag down, and he said, 'HALLO, LOOK KEEN, WHAT'S THIS?'

I said, **'IT'S ME!'**

'AH HA, POPSIE, ON A PROTEST UP THERE, ARE YOU?'

I don't like being called Popsie. Sometimes when Mr Tucker calls me it, I pretend I can't hear him.

But I didn't do that this time because of being stuck out on the window ledge in the dark and the rain and everything, and needing to get rescued.

So I said, '*NO, I'M NOT ON A PROTEST.*' Because I wasn't. '*I'M STUCK.*'

'STUCK, IS IT?'

'*YES,*' I said. '*I CAME OUT AND NOW I CAN'T GET BACK IN.*'

Mr Tucker said, 'NOT BINDING ON?'

And I said, '*WHAT?*'

Because sometimes it's hard to know what Mr Tucker means, with him being from the war and everything.

'COMPLAINING ABOUT THE CONDITIONS?'

'NO,' I said. 'I CAME OUT TO SEE SUZANNE AND THE WINDOW CLOSED BEHIND ME.'

'AH HA, BOTCHED OP, EH? SIT TIGHT, I'LL GET ME KIT.'

And he went and got his long ladder, and he put it up to the window, and held it steady at the bottom, and said, 'THAT'S IT. YOU'VE GOT THE GREEN. CHOCKS AWAY.'

And I climbed down.

I stood behind Mr Tucker, and Mr Tucker rang on our doorbell.

Mum opened the door. And Tom was with her, in his Batman pyjamas, and he was pleased to see Mr Tucker, because talking to Mr Tucker is one of Tom's best things.

191

Tom gave Mr Tucker the salute. And Mr Tucker gave Tom the salute back. Because that's what Tom and Mr Tucker always do when they see each other.

And Mr Tucker said, 'You're in your best blues there, Old Chum. Bang on target, those jimjams. Batman, eh? Smashing, Basher.'

And Tom stuck his chest out.

And Mr Tucker said to Mum, 'Missing one of your mob, Mrs Morris? Found this one trying to bail out.'

And he pointed behind him. I poked my head round.

Mum said, 'Anna, what are you doing? Why are you wet?'

We went inside, and I told Mum about what happened with the Knocking Code, and how

I went out the window, and climbed over to Suzanne's, and how my window closed behind me, and how I couldn't get back in, and how the rain came down, and how I banged on the windows, and shouted for help, and how I climbed all the way down the long ladder by myself.

Mum didn't look very happy. And I thought I was going to be in Big Trouble again because she said, '*Anna...*' the way she always does.

But Mr Tucker butted in. 'What a line!' he said, 'No, no, no. *Here's* how it went. I *smell* something's up, you see - instinct. Go out on me own, no Second Dickey. Clock Popsie, dead ahead, ten angels up and about to bail. Say to myself, "Look lively, Wing Commander, your 12 o'clock, young blonde job doing the dutch!" I get weaving right away. Caught some bad flack off Mrs Tucker,

"RAYMOND!" and all that. Corkscrew out of it. Ladder up. Popsie down. Safe and sound. Spot on (be surprised if I don't get a gong as it goes). No need to debrief Blondie, though, Chiefy. Caught a packet on her way down, lot of offensive fire. Tore a strip off her myself, of course. Badly botched op, and the clot hadn't packed her 'chute correctly. All in order now, though. No harm done. Prob'ly do with a brew up.'

Mum looked at me. I was cold. And I was dripping quite a lot on the carpet. And she started smiling. And Mr Tucker started smiling too. And then Mum and Mr Tucker started laughing. And they got The Hysterics, which is what you get when you start laughing and then you can't stop.

But I didn't get The Hysterics. Because my feet were going blue, and anyway, like Tom said, 'It's not that funny.'

Mum got me a towel, and made some tea.

And Mr Tucker drank his, and said, 'Better get on, or I'll catch another packet off Mrs Tucker. If you fancy pulling your finger out tomorrow, I shall be out plugging away at this litter situation again. Four coke cans, three carrier bags, and a half-eaten carton of chicken chow mein today. Doesn't do, Popsie, doesn't do. O-eight-hundred-hours, eh?'

Normally, I tell Mr Tucker I'm too busy to pick up litter. Especially on a Saturday morning. Because I'd rather watch cartoons, or work on the Super-Speed-Bike-Machine with Suzanne, or sit on the shed roof or something. But seeing as how Mr Tucker had rescued me, I said, 'Okay.'

And Tom said that he was coming too, because he loves doing things with Mr Tucker. Especially picking up litter. He follows him up and down and holds the bin bag open for Mr Tucker to put the rubbish in.

Mr Tucker said, 'Spot on, Tom.' And he messed up Tom's hair. And Tom and Mr Tucker gave each other the salute again.

And then Mr Tucker went home.

Mr Tucker isn't like the people who do rescues in Made-Up Stories or Fairy Tales or anything like that. Because no one ever makes Sleeping Beauty or Rapunzel go on a litter pick.

Anyway, after that I didn't go out on the window ledge again.

The next day, me and Suzanne told Mrs Rotherham all about what happened with Mr Tucker, and the Knocking Code, and how we couldn't go out of our windows to talk anymore. Mrs Rotherham got us some ice cream, and she said, 'Mmm, let me think...' And then she winked. 'I've got just the things for you two if I can lay my hands on them.'

And she went into one of her cupboards.

197

And she found two walkie-talkies. Not toy walkie-talkies like some people have. Real walkie-talkies that Mrs Rotherham used to use when she was in the police. About a million years ago.

Mrs Rotherham cleaned the walkie-talkies up, and got them working, and she gave them to us to keep.

If anything ever happens to my Mum and Dad, I'll probably go and live with Mrs Rotherham, as long as she doesn't mind Tom coming too, even though she's old, and her house smells a bit strange. Because she's got lots of good stuff in her cupboards, and she always gives you ice cream, and she never tells you not to do things.

☙ CHAPTER 3 ☙
The Old Rabbit And The New Cat

Before everything happened with Joe-down-the-road, before he went away, and had to get rescued, I didn't really mind all that much whether he was down the road or not. Because most of the time, when he *was* down the road, Joe just did things on his own. And partly that was because Joe didn't want to do the things me and Suzanne were doing. And partly that was because me and Suzanne didn't want to do the things Joe was doing. But mainly it was because Joe wouldn't come out of his garden because he had to guard his New Rabbit.

Most people who've got rabbits don't really

guard them all that much. Because they probably think that when a rabbit's in its hutch, nothing bad can happen to it. But Joe-down-the-road knows that even in their hutches, rabbits aren't always safe. Because Joe used to have another rabbit, called the *Old* Rabbit, that he got off his Dad, when his Dad still lived at Joe's house, before he went away.

And once, when Joe was playing out the back with me and Suzanne, a cat went in Joe's garden, and looked in at Joe's Old Rabbit, sitting in its hutch. And the Old Rabbit was so scared when it saw the cat that it panicked, and died. And that's why, when Joe's Mum got him a New Rabbit, Joe started guarding it straight away.

Joe's Mum's Boyfriend said, 'The Old Rabbit was daft to die just because a cat *looked* at it.' Because 'It's not like the cat could open the hutch.'

But the Old Rabbit *wasn't* daft really because, like Suzanne said, 'You don't have time to think about things like that when you're about to die of fright.'

And it isn't just rabbits that can die of fright, either. Anyone can. Suzanne knows all about it, after she saw a programme on telly called 'Scared to Death'.

And she said, 'A man died of fright when his wife jumped out on him from inside the wardrobe.'

Which the wife said was meant to be a joke. But like Tom said, 'It wasn't a very funny one.'

Suzanne always gets to watch all the good stuff on telly. Not like me and Tom. My Mum turns it over and puts 'Coronation Street' on instead. When Suzanne told Joe all about the 'Scared to Death' programme, and the man who died of fright, Joe said he was going to jump out on his Mum's Boyfriend from their wardrobe and see if it worked. But he never got the chance because Joe's Mum's Boyfriend stopped being her Boyfriend soon after that. And he started being Joe's Babysitter's Boyfriend instead. And Joe never saw him again.

Joe's got a different babysitter now, called Brian.

Anyway, the thing with Joe's Old Rabbit was, it wasn't just *any* old cat that scared it to death. In fact it wasn't an *old* cat at all. It was a *new* cat. *Our* New Cat, which is a wild cat that we got off a farm. And everyone is scared of it: me, and Mum, and even the Milkman. Because the New Cat is a *mad* cat. And it attacks anything it can. The only one who isn't afraid of the New Cat is Tom.

This is a list me and Suzanne made of all the things that the New Cat has killed…

ANNA'S AND SUZANNE'S LIST OF THINGS THAT THE NEW CAT HAS KILLED

6 mice

2 frogs (one might have been a toad. After the New Cat got it, it was hard to tell)

4 blackbirds

2 jackdaws

1 rat

12 spiders

4 moths

1 shrew

3 bees (the New Cat doesn't even mind when it gets stung)

Whenever the New Cat kills something, me and Suzanne do a funeral for it. We put the body in a box, and we bury it in the back lane. We've buried so many things in our bit of the back lane that we've run out of room. So now we have to bury things in Miss Matheson's bit too. Miss Matheson lives next door, on the other side. Our house is between hers and Suzanne's.

Miss Matheson doesn't like it when she sees me and Suzanne burying things in her bit of the back lane.

She shouts, **'YOU GIRLS GET OUT OF IT! THAT'S MY GARDEN, NOT A**

GRAVEYARD. GET AWAY FROM MY GLADIOLI!'

And she phones Mum to complain.

I think we should be allowed to bury whatever we want in Miss Matheson's bit of the back lane. Because Miss Matheson ran over our Old Cat, which never used to kill anything, and if she hadn't done that, we would never have got the New Cat in the first place. And then it wouldn't be here to keep killing things all the time.

● CHAPTER 4 ●
You Be The Dog

Joe guards the New Rabbit with a Super Soaker
water pistol. Sometimes he marches up and
down in front of the hutch with his Super Soaker.
And sometimes he stands still by the hutch with
his Super Soaker. And sometimes he sits on the
hutch with his Super Soaker. And if anything
comes anywhere near Joe's garden, like a cat, or
a pigeon, or an ant, Joe blasts it and shouts, **'TAKE
THAT! AND DON'T EVER COME
BACK!'**

Before Joe started guarding his rabbit all the time, me and Suzanne and Joe used to do lots of things together, like going on the rope swing at the top of the road, and sliding down the stairs in sleeping bags, and seeing who could hold their breath the longest before they die. And sometimes we played games that everyone knows, like Shops, and Schools, and Prisons, and things. And sometimes we played our own made-up games, like Dingo the Dog, and Mountain Rescue, and breaking the world record on the Super-Speed-Bike-Machine.

Here's what happens in Dingo the Dog. There's a school, for dogs, and Suzanne is the teacher. (Suzanne knows all about dog schools because she used to take her dog Barney to one, before her Dad said he was allergic and sent Barney to live on a farm.) Anyway, Suzanne tells all the dogs what to do, like 'Stay,' and 'Roll over,' and 'Heel,' and all that. (There aren't real dogs in the class. We just pretend. There's only one real dog in our road, and it belongs to Miss Matheson. It's the same size as a guinea pig, and we aren't allowed to play with it.)

Anyway, there are lots of pretend dogs in the class, and they're all doing what they are told. And I come to the class with my dog, which is a bad dog called Dingo (it's really Joe-down-the-road, on his hands and knees, with Barney's old collar on and a lead.) And Dingo goes around sniffing all the other dogs, and Suzanne tells him off. And then Dingo spots a dog he really hates, and he barks, and goes crazy, and slips his collar off, and chases the dog around the room, and right out of the class. And I run up and down the road shouting, **'Dingo, Dingo, here boy!'** and try to get him back. But Dingo hides in the bushes, and howls, and tears up the flowerbeds, and wees up trees and everything. And all the other dogs in the class go mad and start chasing each other too. And their owners complain, and ask Suzanne for their money back.

It's a pretty good game.

But it's no good without Joe because no one else can do Dingo. Because Suzanne is only good at telling the dogs what to do. And I'm only good at doing the chasing. And once Tom tried to be Dingo, but he didn't like the lead, and he wasn't any good at being bad. Because he just sat when Suzanne told him to sit, and stayed when she told him to stay. And then, when Suzanne told him he was supposed to be a *bad* dog, he bit her. On the arm. Really hard. And Suzanne screamed. And went home. And Tom had to go in the house and sit with Mum and have a biscuit.

And Mum took Tom off the lead, and said, 'Best not to play Dingo the Dog anymore, Anna.'

Another game we used to play with Joe-down-the-road is the Mountain Rescue Game. We play it inside when it's really raining, and we aren't allowed out. We don't play it in Suzanne's house, though, not since her Dad tripped over the rescue rope, and went flying down the stairs, and said, **'THIS IS A STAIRCASE, SUZANNE, NOT SNOWDONIA! YOU CHILDREN COULD'VE KILLED ME!'**

Anyway, what happens in Mountain Rescue is, Suzanne goes to the top of the stairs, which is the top of the mountain, because she's best at screaming for help and dangling from the banisters and everything. And me and Joe have to rescue her, and we're tied together with ropes (it used to be real ropes but Mum took them away, so now we get tied together with Mum's tights instead). And Joe has his stopwatch, and he keeps looking at it and saying, 'She's only got two minutes of air left at the top before she dies.' And things like that.

And then we start climbing up, which takes ages

because it's all windy and icy and high. And Joe says, 'We're approaching the summit.'

And then he says, **'AVALANCHE!'**

And that's when we fall all the way down. And land at the bottom. And then we have to climb all the way back up again. In the end we bring Suzanne down on a stretcher, which is a sleeping bag. And sometimes she's alive, and other times she's dead. We don't do the Mountain Rescue Game anymore though because Joe's the only one with a stop-watch, and last time, when me and Suzanne played Mountain Rescue on our own, when I got to the top, we fell out about whether Suzanne was dead or not. Because Suzanne said she was, even though she wasn't. And she wouldn't help me get her down the mountain. And that's why the stretcher slipped and Suzanne went all the way down on her own, and landed on her head. And then she went home.

And Mum said, 'Best not to play Mountain Rescue anymore, Anna.'

And we aren't allowed on the Super-Speed-Bike-Machine anymore either. The Super-Speed-Bike-Machine is my bike, with Joe's stunt pegs on the back wheel for standing on, and Tom's old stabilisers on the sides, and Suzanne's trailer tied on behind. Before Joe's Dad stopped living at Joe's house, me and Suzanne and Joe-down-the-road used to work on the Super-Speed-Bike-Machine all the time, cleaning it, and putting spokies on the wheels, and streamers on the handlebars, and stickers on the crossbar, and painting the trailer, and pumping up the tyres, and repairing the punctures, and all that.

And after we worked on it, we would take it right up to the top of the back lane, by Miss Matheson's garden, which used to drive her dog mad, and Miss Matheson would run out and shout, 'YOU KIDS GET THAT CONTRAPTION AWAY FROM MY GATE!'

And then I would get on the seat, and Suzanne would sit on the handlebars, and Joe would stand on the stunt pegs, and Tom would kneel in the trailer, and Joe's Dad would stand at the bottom of the back lane. And we'd all say, **'THREE, TWO, ONE, BLAST OFF!'**

And then Joe pushed off from the stunt pegs, and Suzanne leaned back, and Tom held tight to the trailer, and I pedalled my fastest, and we all went flying down the back lane, over the hump, right to the bottom, where Joe put his foot out to slow the Super-Speed-Bike-Machine down, and Joe's Dad grabbed hold to stop us going into the road. And then we checked the seconds on the stopwatch and, if it was a world record, we put it in the record book. And if it wasn't, we went all the way back up to the top, and did it again. And sometimes we did it all day.

Once, after Joe's Dad stopped living at Joe's house, and Joe's Old Rabbit died, and Joe started guarding his New Rabbit all the time, me and Suzanne and Tom went on the Super-Speed-Bike-Machine on our own. But Joe wasn't there to put his foot out at the end to slow us down, and his Dad wasn't there to grab the Super-Speed-Bike-Machine and stop it going in the road, and it did go in the road, and it only stopped when it hit the kerb on the other side, and then Tom flew out of the trailer, and the Super-Speed-Bike-Machine went over on its side, and a van had to screech to a stop. And Tom had to go to hospital and get six sticky stitches in his head.

And Mum said, 'Best not to go on the Super-Speed-Bike-Machine again, Anna.'

And she put it at the back of the shed, under an old sheet,

behind the stepladders, and the garden canes, and the broken old floorboards.

Anyway, when Joe first started guarding the New Rabbit, me and Suzanne sometimes used to go and guard it with him. Joe told us all the rules, and we took our Super Soakers and we marched up and down and blasted anything that moved. But after a while, especially when nothing much came except squirrels and starlings and daddy-long-legs and things, me and Suzanne got sick of guarding the New Rabbit.

And we said, 'Let's go and do something else, like make plans, or do Dizzy Ducklings, or sit on the shed roof instead.'

But Joe always said, 'No.'

And one day, when Tom came to guard the New Rabbit with us, Joe said that Tom wasn't allowed in his garden because of him liking the New Cat. And he blasted Tom with the Super Soaker and said, 'Take that! And don't ever come back!'

And Tom fell over. And he ran up the road. And me and Joe fell out after that. And Joe's Mum sent me home. And I got in Big Trouble. Even though it was Joe's fault in the first place because, like I said, 'It's not Tom's fault that the New Cat is his friend!'

But Mum said she didn't care because, 'Whatever happens, Anna, you don't beat people about the head with Super Soakers.'

And after that I didn't go and see Joe-down-the-road and guard the New Rabbit much anymore. Apart from when Mum made me. Because I'd rather do other things. Like going on the walkie-talkies, or doing funerals, or finding woodlice.

And, anyway, me and Suzanne had our clubs to do, which no one else was allowed in.

ANNA'S AND SUZANNE'S CLUBS THAT NO ONE ELSE (EXCEPT SOMETIMES TOM) IS ALLOWED IN

1. Shed Club

Make up a password

Don't let anyone in who doesn't know the password (except Tom when he forgets it)

Make plans

Don't tell anyone the plans

2. Worm Club

Collect worms

Put the worms in the worm box in the shed

Write down how many worms there are in the record book (most number of worms in a day so far = 43)

3. Bug Club

Same as Worm Club but with bugs instead of worms

Cover the bugs with a lid or they get away

Put holes in the lid or they die

4. Spy Club

Spy on people with the binoculars Mrs Rotherham
gave us

Write what people are up to in the notepad

People we have got pages on in the notepad are...

1. Miss Matheson

2. The Lollipop Lady

3. Mr Tucker

4. Suzanne's Dad

5. Joe's Mum

6. Joe's Mum's Old
Boyfriend

7. Joe's Old Babysitter

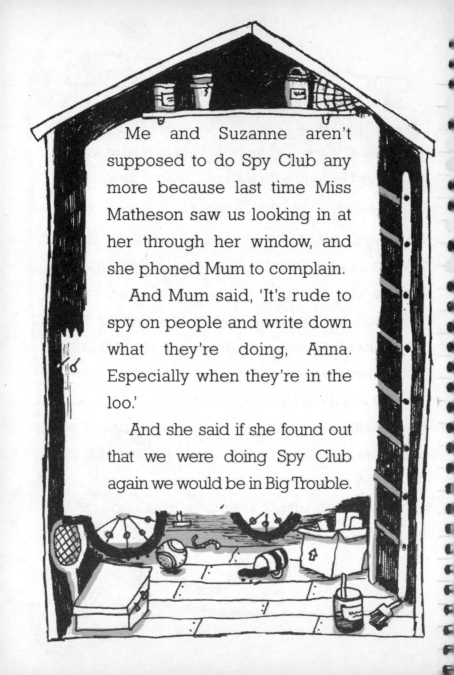

Me and Suzanne aren't supposed to do Spy Club any more because last time Miss Matheson saw us looking in at her through her window, and she phoned Mum to complain.

And Mum said, 'It's rude to spy on people and write down what they're doing, Anna. Especially when they're in the loo.'

And she said if she found out that we were doing Spy Club again we would be in Big Trouble.

So we put the binoculars and the notepad away, at the back of the shed, on the shelf above the broken floorboards and the stepladders and the Super-Speed-Bike-Machine.

Sometimes Tom does clubs with me and Suzanne, except Worm Club because he says worms wriggle his skin, but most of the time he forgets he's meant to be looking for weevils and woodlice and things, and goes to see Mum and get a biscuit, or to talk to Mr Tucker about his old sports car instead. Doing clubs is pretty good, and so is sitting on the shed roof, and going on the walkie-talkies and things, but not as good as before, when Joe didn't have to guard his rabbit, and Joe's Dad was still in the road, and we did Dingo the Dog, and Mountain Rescue, and going on the Super-Speed-Bike-Machine.

CHAPTER 5
A Rabbit Pie Chart

Joe couldn't guard his New Rabbit *all* the time though, because, like his Mum said, 'Sometimes you have to do other things, Joe, like sleep, and eat, and go to school.'

But whenever he *wasn't* doing those sorts of things, Joe stayed in his garden because he said, 'The less time the New Rabbit gets guarded, the more chance there is of the New Rabbit getting got.'

Which is probably true.

But some people didn't think Joe needed to guard his New Rabbit at all. Mrs Peters told Joe that she didn't think so, the day we made pie chart mobiles at school.

That morning, Mrs Peters said, 'Right, everyone, here is a sum. There are twenty-four hours in a day. If Janet spends ten hours in bed, and six hours at school, how many hours has Janet got left for doing other things?'

And she wrote it on the white board. Some people put their hands up, like Emma Hendry, but not Joe because, even though Joe is good at sums, he isn't very good at putting his hand up. Which is different to Emma Hendry. Because Emma Hendry is good at putting her hand up, but she isn't very good at sums.

Anyway, even though Joe didn't put his hand up, Mrs Peters said, 'Joe, why don't you have a go?'

And Joe said, 'Twenty-four hours take away ten hours sleeping equals fourteen hours; and fourteen hours take away six hours at school equals eight hours, so Janet's got eight hours left to do what she wants.'

And he said it really fast. Just like that. And he was right because Mrs Peters said, 'Very good. Well done, Joe.'

And she wrote it on the board like this:

$$24 - 10 = 14$$
$$14 - 6 = 8$$

I didn't get that answer. I didn't get any answer, because for one thing I'm even worse at sums than Emma Hendry is, especially if I have to do them in my head. And for another thing, Mrs Peters said here is *a* sum and that was actually *two* sums. And for an even other thing, Graham Roberts, who sits next to me, drew a picture in his book of a girl called Janet. And he drew some fumes coming off Janet's bum and he wrote, Janet has eight hours a day to drop bum bombs. And I got The Hysterics. And Mrs Peters said I had to go and stand outside the classroom and do deep breathing until I calmed down.

When I came back, Mrs Peters drew a big circle on the white board, and she said that the circle was 'a day'. And she drew twenty-four slices in the circle, which was 'one for each hour'. And she coloured some of the slices in to show the different things Janet did in a day. And she said it was called a 'pie chart'.

This is what Mrs Peters's pie chart of Janet's day looked like:

JANET'S DAY →

8 hrs left to do what she wants

z z z z z z z z z z
SLEEPING z
z z z z z
z z z z

SCHOOL

In the afternoon, Mrs Peters helped us all do our own pie charts. And we could put anything we liked in them. Mine was like this:

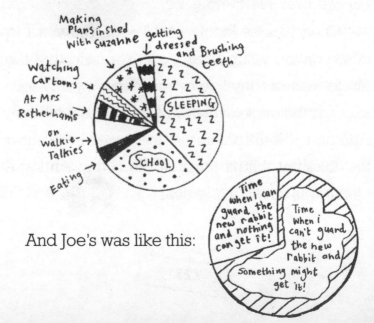

Making Plans in shed With Suzanne

getting dressed

and Brushing teeth

Watching Cartoons →

At Mrs Rotherham's →

on walkie-Talkies →

Eating →

z z z z z z z z z
SLEEPING
z z z z z
z z z z z
SCHOOL z

And Joe's was like this:

Time when i can guard the new rabbit and nothing can get it!

Time when i can't guard the new rabbit and something might get it!

Later on we coloured our pie charts in. Mrs Peters said our pie charts were so good, she was going to cut them out, and put a string through each one, and hang them from the ceiling to make mobiles. Emma Hendry asked Mrs Peters why pie charts are called pie charts. And Mrs Peters said it's because they look like pies. Which is true. They don't taste like pies, though, because Graham Roberts licked his. And he got blue felt-tip all over his tongue. And I got The Hysterics again. And Mrs Peters sent me back out of the classroom. And Graham Roberts had to put his tongue under the tap.

When the bell went, Mrs Peters said she wanted to talk to Joe about his pie chart, and some other work he'd done, like his poem about the rabbit that dies when it gets dark, and his story about the rabbit that can't get to sleep, and his painting of the rabbit being guarded with guns. Me and Suzanne stayed behind to wait for Joe, to walk home. Mrs Peters told Joe he wasn't in trouble. She said she just wondered whether he might be worried about something. Like his rabbit, maybe.

Joe told Mrs Peters that he wasn't worried. And Mrs Peters asked if he was sure.

And Joe said, 'Yes.'

And Mrs Peters said that that was good. Because she didn't think that Joe needed to worry about his rabbit. Because she thought his rabbit was very safe.

'Because,' she said, 'rabbits are pretty tough, you know, Joe.'

And Joe said, 'I know.'

Even though he didn't really think so.

Mrs Peters asked me and Suzanne what we thought.

And I said, '*Some* rabbits are tough.'

And Suzanne said, 'Joe's Old Rabbit wasn't. It got scared to death by Anna's Cat.'

'Did it?' said Mrs Peters.

And Suzanne said, 'Yes.'

And Mrs Peters asked, 'How?'

And Suzanne told her, 'In its hutch.'

'Oh. I see. That's not very nice, is it?'

And Suzanne said, 'No.'

Because it wasn't. Especially not for Joe. Or the Old Rabbit.

Mrs Peters asked, 'Do you want to tell me about your Old Rabbit, Joe?'

And Joe said, 'No.'

233

And Mrs Peters said, 'Okay'.

And then she said that she thought that what had happened to Joe's Old Rabbit was 'very sad and very bad luck'. But she didn't think that it meant that something bad was going to happen to Joe's *New* Rabbit. Because she thought that it was 'a one-off'. Which is when something only happens once. And then she said, 'Lightning doesn't strike twice, as they say'.

Joe didn't say anything.

Mrs Peters said, 'What do you think, Joe?'

And Joe said, 'Okay'.

And Mrs Peters smiled at Joe, 'Okay, then.' And she gave him a stroke on the head, which Mrs Peters doesn't normally do. And then she said, 'Have a good weekend.' Because it was Friday. And me and Suzanne and Joe walked home.

On the way, I asked Joe if he was going to stop guarding his New Rabbit now.

And Joe said, 'No. Mrs Peters is wrong about lightning not striking twice, because there was a man in America called Roy Sullivan who got struck by lightning seven times.'

And that's true, because I looked on the computer when I got home and, before he died, Roy Sullivan was always getting struck by lightning. And his wife got struck by lightning too. So if anyone ever says that lightning doesn't strike twice, they're wrong. Because sometimes it does. And sometimes it strikes seven times, like it did with Roy Sullivan. And that's why they called him 'The Human Light Bulb'.

235

I told Suzanne what it said on the computer about people getting struck by lightning millions of times and everything. And about Roy Sullivan. And how he was the human light bulb and all that. And I said, 'Want to see?'

And Suzanne said, 'No.'

And I said, 'Oh.'

And Suzanne said, 'I already know.'

Suzanne always says she already knows when you try to tell her things.

I said, 'Well, Roy Sullivan and his wife aren't the only ones because there are lots of people who've got struck by lightning twice, like his wife, and lots of trees too.'

And Suzanne said, 'I know' again.

And I said, 'No, you don't.'

Because she didn't.

And Suzanne said she did know actually, and even if she *didn't* know, she didn't care. Because what she *really* didn't know was why everyone kept going on about lightning all the time. Like me, and Joe, and Mrs Peters.

Because, she said, 'Lightning hasn't even got anything to do with it because it isn't lightning that Joe is guarding the New Rabbit from. It's other things, like cats!'

I said I wouldn't show Suzanne anything on the computer ever again. Or tell her any more things about anything. Especially not Roy Sullivan. Not even if she asked.

‟ CHAPTER 6 ‟
Joe-Down-The-Road's Dad's Van

Sometimes, me and Suzanne go down the bottom of the back lane, and we take the walkie-talkies, and we stand back to back. And Suzanne walks *down* the road, and I walk *up* the road, because we want to know how far apart we can go before the walkie-talkies stop working. When we've gone twenty steps apart, we stop, and Suzanne says, 'Suzanne to Anna. Suzanne to Anna. Come in, Anna. I'm at the pet shop. What's your position? Over.'

And I say, 'Anna to Suzanne. Anna to Suzanne. I'm at the conker tree. Over.'

And then Suzanne says, 'Copy that.

Conker tree. Are you receiving me? Over.'

And I say, 'Yes. Over.'

And then Suzanne says, 'You're supposed to say, "Receiving you loud and clear. Over".'

And I say, 'Oh. Receiving you loud and clear. Over.'

And Suzanne says, 'Copy that. Over and out.'

And then we walk twenty more steps apart, and say the same stuff again, about where we are, and whether we can hear each other and everything. Only I don't always do all the 'Come ins', and the 'Copies', and the 'Over and outs' and all that, even though Suzanne says her uncle in the army said you should. Because sometimes I forget. And sometimes it takes too long. And sometimes I'd rather say something else instead.

Once, when me and Suzanne were seeing how far apart we could go, I got all the way down to the Bottom Bus Stop, and Suzanne got all the way up to the Police Station. Which are *ages* apart from each other, at opposite ends of the village, and the walkie-talkies still worked. But that's as far apart as we've got, because Suzanne's not allowed past the Police Station, or the Bottom Bus Stop, because her Dad says it's **'OUT OF BOUNDS!'**

I don't know if I'm allowed past the Police Station or the Bottom Bus Stop or not. My Dad has never said anything about bounds to me before. I probably am though. I'm normally allowed to do more things than Suzanne. Because even though Suzanne's Mum doesn't mind Suzanne doing most things, like going out of the back lane, or not taking a coat, or doing relay races up the road in bare feet, Suzanne's Dad minds Suzanne doing a *lot* of things. And if it was only up to him, Suzanne probably wouldn't be allowed to do anything at all. Except eat her tea, and brush her teeth, and go to bed, and things like that. Suzanne's Dad is different to my Dad. If you ask my Dad if you can do something he says, 'You can play on the A1 as far as I'm concerned, Anna. But you'd better ask your Mum.'

But Suzanne's Dad just says, **'NO!'**

And he's not the sort of Dad you can say, 'Ahhhh, but whyyYYYyy though, Dad, PleeEEase?' to. Because he won't change his

241

mind. He'll only say, **'RIGHT, THAT'S IT. ROOM!'**

Anyway, this time we didn't get anywhere near the Bottom Bus Stop and the Police Station because we were just standing back to back, at the bottom of our road, ready to go, when we saw Joe's Dad's van coming.

We knew it was Joe's Dad's van because it said, *Barry Walker: Small Building Works, Renovation and Refurbishment* on the side.

The van stopped right outside Joe's house, where it always used to stop when Joe's Dad still lived there. So me and Suzanne stopped doing the walkie-talkie testing, and decided to do some spying instead. Because, even though we aren't supposed to do Spy Club anymore because Mum says we're banned, sometimes we *have* to do it if it's really important.

Suzanne ran up the road and got the binoculars, and the notepad, and we turned the walkie-talkies off, and crouched down low behind a car at the bottom of the road. Suzanne looked round from behind the car through the binoculars.

'What can you see?' I said.

'Joe's Dad's hair.'

Suzanne passed the binoculars to me.

She was right. You *could* see Joe's Dad's hair.

And you couldn't see much else. Because for one thing we were too close to Joe's Dad to really need the binoculars. Because the whole point of binoculars is that they are for looking at things that are far away. And for another thing, Joe's Dad has got a lot of hair. It's long and brown and curly.

'He's got split ends,' Suzanne said. 'And he's going grey.' She wrote in the notepad: Saturday, 9.45am. Joe's Dad outside Joe's house in his van.

And then she put: Split ends. Going grey.

Suzanne knows all about hair because her Mum is a hairdresser.

Suzanne's Mum cut Joe's Dad's hair when he still lived in our road. When Joe's Dad stopped living in our road, Suzanne's Mum said to my Mum, 'What a shame.'

And my Mum said, 'I know. Such a lovely man.'

And Suzanne's Mum said, 'And such lovely hair.'

And my Mum said, 'Yeah.'

And they both shook their heads for ages.

Suzanne's Mum cuts my Dad's hair too, and Suzanne's Dad's. She doesn't say *they've* got lovely hair though. My Dad and Suzanne's Dad are bald.

Anyway, Joe's Dad got out of his van and he

went round to the back of it, and opened the van doors, and took out three big brown boxes, and he carried the boxes up the path to Joe's house and he rang on Joe's doorbell, and went inside.

Suzanne wrote down: 9.48am. Joe's Dad takes three big brown boxes into Joe's house.

'Maybe Joe's Dad has come back to live at Joe's house,' said Suzanne.

And I said I hoped he had. Because then he would fix the rope swing at the top of the road, where the rope was caught up and the tyre had come off.

Joe's Dad is good at fixing things. He can fix bikes and binoculars and buildings and everything. He fixed our shed roof after I fell through it, so me and Suzanne could sit on it again.

And he's good at other things too. Like teaching you how to do relay races, and pushing you round in his wheelbarrow, and getting you with the hosepipe when he's cleaning his van.

When Joe's Dad stopped living down the road, me and Tom asked our Dad if *he* would get us with the hosepipe. Dad said, 'Why not cut out the middle man? Stick your heads under the outside tap if you want to get wet.'

'*Joe's* Dad gets us with the hosepipe,' I said. 'It's fun.'

'Yeah yeah yeah,' Dad said. 'I used to be fun. And I used to have hair.'

I asked Dad when his hair fell out.

Dad said, 'The day you were born.' And then he laughed. Even though it wasn't funny.

Tom told Dad, 'Joe-down-the-road's Dad has got hair, and a van, and a cement mixer, and that's why he's the best Dad in the road.'

'Right!' Dad said. And he grabbed Tom and tickled him. But not for long because if you tickle Tom too much he wets himself. And then he gets upset. And also because the football came on. And Dad doesn't do anything when that happens. Except drink his beer, and shout at the telly, and put his hands over his eyes.

Anyway, me and Suzanne were crouching quietly behind the car at the bottom of the road, waiting to see what happened.

And then Tom came running down the road, and he saw us and he shouted, **'WHAT ARE YOU DOING?'**

'Shh,' I said, 'we're spying. Get down.'

And Tom got down behind the car as well.

Joe's Dad came out of Joe's house, holding one of the big brown boxes. He went round to the back of the van, and he opened the doors, and put the box in the van.

And Tom stood up and he said, 'Hello.'

Joe's Dad looked around to see where the voice had come from.

'Tom!' I whispered. 'Get down!'

249

But he didn't. Tom doesn't really care about spying. He cares more about other things, like Joe's Dad's van.

'Hello, lad,' said Joe's Dad.

'Can I go in your van?' Tom said.

'Ah, not today, Tommy.'

'Why?' Tom said.

Because that's Tom's best question. And because Joe's Dad always used to let him get in his van, and look at all the tools and once let Tom put sand in the cement mixer. And that was about the best thing Tom had ever done. Except for when Mr Tucker let Tom sit on his knee in the driver's seat of his old sports car and put his driving gloves and goggles on. And drive up and down the road, and honk the horn.

Anyway, Joe's Dad said, 'Bit busy today. Next time, eh, Tom? Promise.'

And Tom said, 'Okay.'

And they shook on it. And Joe's Dad went back into Joe's house. And Tom went to talk to Mr Tucker. Mr Tucker is never too busy. Especially not for Tom.

Me and Suzanne stayed waiting. After a while, Joe's Dad came out of Joe's house again with another brown box. And he went round the back of the van, and opened the doors, and put it in. And then he went back into the house, and got the last brown box and put that in the van too. He shut the van doors. And got in the van himself.

And then Joe and his Mum came out of the house. And Joe went over to his rabbit hutch, and he checked the latch, and arranged his plastic soldiers on the roof, and then he got his Super Soaker, and he pumped it up, and blasted some ants. And then he gave his Mum a cuddle. And he got in the van, in the front, next to his Dad. And he put his seatbelt on. And then he took his seatbelt off again, and he got out of the van. And he went over to the rabbit hutch. And checked the latch again. And rearranged his plastic soldiers.

And then Joe's Dad got out of the van too.

And he talked to Joe's Mum for a bit, and he gave Joe a cuddle. And then Joe's Dad got back in the van by himself. And he drove away.

And Joe ran out of his garden, down the road after the van. And the van stopped. And Joe got in it. And the van drove off. And Joe looked out the window. Me and Suzanne waved at Joe, but Joe didn't wave back.

When Joe and Joe's Dad and the van were gone, Joe's Mum sat down on the doorstep by herself. Suzanne looked through the binoculars. And she wrote in the book: 10.45am. Joe-down-the-road's Mum sits down on the step and cries.

CHAPTER 7
The Tale Of Peter Rabbit

Me and Suzanne told my Mum all about Joe's Dad, and his van, and Joe, and the boxes.

Mum said, 'Oh, poor Pam.' (Which is Joe's Mum's name.)

I asked, 'Why?'

'Never mind,' Mum said. 'I'm popping down the road.'

'What for?'

'Nothing.'

'Are you going to spy?' asked Suzanne.

'No, Suzanne,' Mum said, 'I am not going to spy. I'm just going to see Joe's Mum.'

And I said, 'We'll come.'

'No,' Mum said, 'you won't.'

Suzanne asked Mum, 'Why?'

'Because I want to talk to Pam on my own,' Mum said. And off she went.

When Mum came back, after ages, me and Suzanne were waiting for her on the garden wall.

'Where has Joe gone?' I asked.

Mum said, 'To stay with his Dad.'

Me and Suzanne followed Mum into the house.

Suzanne asked, 'Where's that?'

'Not far,' Mum said. 'At his flat.'

'In the village?' I asked.

And Mum said, 'Not quite. Over the bridge.'

Which *is* far. It's ages. Because you have to go on the bus, or at least on a bike.

'Why has he gone?' Suzanne asked.

And Mum said, 'I don't know.'

I asked, 'How long has he gone for?'

And Mum said, 'I don't know.'

And Suzanne said, 'What about his rabbit?'

And Mum said, 'For goodness' sake, girls, I don't *know!*'

And I told Mum she should have let me and Suzanne go with her to Joe's house, because she had hardly found out anything about Joe, or his rabbit. Because she hadn't asked the right questions. And she probably only asked Joe's Mum about work, and the weather, and washing, and things like that.

So I said, 'Come on, Suzanne.'

And Mum said, 'Where are you going?'

And I said, 'To see Joe-down-the-road's Mum to ask her when Joe will be coming back, and what is going to happen with his rabbit while he's gone, of course.'

And Mum said, 'No, Anna, you are not. Here, have an ice pop. Go out the back. And don't bother anyone, *especially* not Joe's Mum.'

So me and Suzanne went outside with our ice pops. And we climbed up on the shed roof, and ate them up there. And when they were finished, we lay flat on our backs to see how long we could stare at the sun. Graham Roberts says if you stare straight at the sun you go blind. But me and Suzanne tried it one day, at exactly the same time, so that if we did go blind it would be together. And afterwards we could still see fine. When we told Graham Roberts, he said we mustn't have stared for long enough.

Anyway, we didn't stare very long this time because there were too many clouds so it didn't count. So we sat up and dangled our legs over the edge of the shed instead. And we tried to think of things to do. Which was hard, because the rope swing was broken and we weren't allowed to do Spy Club or Mountain Rescue, or Dingo the Dog, or go on the Super-Speed-Bike-Machine. And we were sick of doing Worm Club and Bug Club and Shed Club and all that.

Suzanne said she wondered what Joe was doing now. And I said I wondered too. Because even though we hadn't done anything with Joe for ages, I didn't really mind not doing things with Joe when I knew that he was down the road, guarding his rabbit. But now that I didn't know *what* Joe was doing, or when he was coming back, I couldn't stop wondering. Like when Mum gave my old teddy to Mrs Constantine for the Sunday School Jumble Sale. Because before she gave it away, I forgot I even had it. But afterwards I kept thinking about the teddy all the time, and how it was mine, and how it was meant to be in my toy-box, and how I wanted it back.

Suzanne said we should never have told my Mum about Joe's Dad and his van and the boxes and all that. Because before we told her, we could have gone and asked Joe's Mum whatever questions we wanted. But now we couldn't because Mum had said we were banned.

We got down off the shed because it was starting to rain. And we went inside the shed, and sat on the boxes, and listened to the rain on the roof, and wondered about Joe, and what he was up to, and whether anything bad had happened to his rabbit since he had gone. And I said I thought it probably hadn't, because Joe only went about an hour ago, and Suzanne said I was probably right, but it would be nice to know for certain. Which was true. Then there was a knock on the shed door.

Suzanne looked through the spy-hole (which is a knot in the wood that you can pop in and out).

'It's Tom,' she said.

Tom put his eye to the spy hole and said, 'Hello.'

Suzanne said, 'What's the password?'

'I don't know,' said Tom. 'What is it?'

And then me and Suzanne remembered we had forgotten to make one up. Which we never normally do because making up the password is the first rule of Shed Club.

So Suzanne told Tom to guess.

And Tom guessed, 'Open sesame.'

Which is what he always says, and Suzanne said, 'Yes.'

And Tom was very pleased, because 'Open sesame' had never been right before.

We let Tom in, and we told him all about Joe, and how he had got in the van with his Dad, and the boxes, and how he got out again. And how his Dad had driven away. And how Joe chased his Dad down the road. And how they drove away together. And how he didn't take his rabbit with him. And how Mum said Joe had gone to stay with his Dad, in a flat, over the bridge. And how we didn't know why, or for how long, or what was going to happen to Joe's rabbit. And Suzanne said that she didn't think Joe wanted to go. And I said that he didn't want to leave his rabbit.

And Tom said, 'Joe didn't want to go, and he didn't want to leave his rabbit, but he really really really didn't want to be left behind.'

And Tom was probably right because being left behind is one of Tom's worst things, so he knows all about it.

Because, when Tom was little, if Mum wanted to go somewhere without him, Dad had to take

Tom out of the house first so that Tom was the one doing the leaving, not the one being left. Otherwise, if Tom was in the house, and he found out that Mum had gone somewhere and left him behind, he would stand at the door and look through the letterbox and cry until she came home.

But the thing about taking Tom out, even just to the shops, is that you have to do a lot of other things on the way, like talking to Mr Tucker, and walking on the wall, and wetting your wellies in the horse trough. So that's why, if Mum only wants to buy an onion or something, she tries to sneak out before Tom notices.

And then she runs down the road as fast as she can. Most of the time Mum doesn't get that far though because, like she says, 'Tom has got supersonic ears.' And he nearly always hears the door handle turn, even from upstairs.

And then he runs down, quick, and puts his wellies on, and says, 'Are you going out?'

And Mum says, 'Oh, for goodness sake, Tom, I'm only going to get an onion.'

And Tom says, 'I'll come.'

And she has to take him with her. Because if

she doesn't, Tom gets what Nanna used to call 'The Screaming Habdabs' where he screams, and cries, and bangs his fists on the door, and dribbles all over the doormat.

Anyway, me and Suzanne told Tom how we wanted to know why Joe had gone to his Dad's, and when he was coming back, and what was going to happen to his rabbit while he was gone. And how we couldn't ask Joe's Mum about it, because Mum had said we were banned.

And Tom said, '*I'm* not banned.'

Which was true. So we decided that Tom should go instead. And Suzanne said we better make sure Tom knew exactly what to ask Joe's Mum first, before he went. And she wrote it all down in the notepad.

1. Why has Joe gone to his Dad's?
2. When is Joe coming back?
3. What is going to happen to Joe's rabbit?

Tom looked at the list for a while and then he said, 'What does it say?'

Because even though Tom goes to school, and he knows all his letters, he's only in Reception, and he doesn't really know what the letters say when you put them all together. So I said that Suzanne should just tell Tom what to say, and

Tom would remember. And Tom said that was a good idea because even though he isn't a very good *reader* yet, he is a *very* good rememberer. So that is what we did.

'Right,' Suzanne said, 'the shed is Joe's house, and Anna is Joe's Mum.'

And Tom had to go out of the shed and knock on the door. And I answered it as Joe's Mum. And Suzanne told Tom exactly what he should say. And this is how it went:

Tom: 'Hello.'

Me being Joe's Mum: 'Hello.'

Tom: 'How are you?'

Me being Joe's Mum: 'Fine.'

Tom: 'Why has Joe gone to his Dad's?'

Me being Joe's Mum: 'For a holiday.'

Tom: 'When will he be coming back?'

267

Me being Joe's Mum: 'On Thursday.'

Tom: 'What about his rabbit?'

Me being Joe's Mum: 'He will be back in a minute to take it with him.'

Tom: 'Thank you, Joe's Mum. Bye.'

We practiced it again and again. And Suzanne told me to say different answers every time because she said, 'Who knows what answers Joe's Mum might say.'

Which was true. And she said it was best for Tom to get used to Joe's Mum saying all sorts of answers so he wouldn't get flustered and forget everything if she said something he didn't expect. We practised it over and over again until Tom said all the questions exactly right, every time.

And, after about a million times, Suzanne said, 'Tom is ready.'

And Tom was pleased, because he said, 'I'm a *very* good rememberer.'

And we went off down the road.

Tom knocked on Joe's door. And me and Suzanne crouched behind the hedge.

And Joe's Mum answered the door and said, 'Hello, Tom.' Just like we thought.

And Tom said, 'Hello, Joe's Mum. How are you?' Just like he was supposed to.

And Joe's Mum said, 'Oh, I don't know, Tom, not very good.'

And Tom said, 'Oh.'

And then he said, 'Can I have a biscuit?'

Which he was not supposed to say.

And Joe's Mum said, 'Umm… Have you had your lunch?'

And Tom said, 'No.'

And Joe's Mum said, 'You shouldn't really.'

And Tom said, 'Just a plain one.'

And Joe's Mum said, 'Okay.'

And she went in the house and she brought the biscuits out and she said, 'Shall I have one with you?'

And Tom said, 'Have you had your lunch?'

And Joe's Mum said, 'No.'

And Tom said, 'Okay.'

And they sat down on the doorstep. And they got a biscuit each. And Tom had a bite of his biscuit. And Joe's Mum had a bite of her biscuit. And Tom had a bite of his biscuit. And Joe's Mum had a bite of her biscuit. And they took turns having bites like that until their biscuits were finished.

And then Tom said, 'Shall we have a story?'

And Joe's Mum said, 'Okay.'

And she went and got some books, and Tom picked *Peter Rabbit* because he said, '*Peter Rabbit* is one of my best.'

And Joe's Mum said it was one of Joe's best too, when he was Tom's age. And they sat on the step. And Joe's Mum read *Peter Rabbit*. And when it was finished, they had another biscuit, and they took it in turn to have bites.

And then Tom said, 'Shall we have *Peter Rabbit* again?'

And Joe's Mum said, 'Alright.'

And she read *Peter Rabbit* again. And she cuddled Tom in, and rubbed her cheek on his head. When the story was finished, Tom said, 'That was nice.'

And Joe's Mum said, 'Yes.'

And Tom said, 'I'm going home now.'

And Joe's Mum said, 'Okay.'

And she brushed the biscuit crumbs off Tom, and off herself. And she smiled and said, 'Don't tell about the biscuits.' And she put her finger over her mouth. And Tom put his finger over his mouth too. And he walked down the path, and back up the road.

And me and Suzanne followed, and I said, 'Tom! You didn't ask why Joe has gone to his Dad's, and when he's coming back, and what's going to happen with his rabbit!'

And Tom said, 'I forgot to remember. I had a story instead.'

And I said, *'Tom!'*

And Tom said, 'I didn't have biscuits.'

And then he said, 'Joe's Mum cried on my head.'

And she had as well, because Tom's hair was all wet.

Me and Suzanne went back to the shed and decided to wait until tomorrow at school, when we could ask *Joe* why he had gone to his Dad's, and when he was coming back, and what was going to happen with his rabbit.

CHAPTER 8

The Spare Seat

Most of the time, I'm not very good at getting ready in the mornings. And that's why Mum always shouts things up the stairs like, 'Anna, if you don't hurry up, I'm going to come up there and dress you myself.'

But the morning after Joe-down-the-road went away with his Dad in the van, I got ready really fast. And I packed my bag and got my uniform ready the night before. Because, like Suzanne said, 'We have to get there early to talk to Joe before the bell goes.'

I was eating my breakfast when the walkie-talkie crackled, 'Suzanne to Anna. Suzanne to

Anna. Are you ready? Over.'

'Anna to Suzanne. Anna to Suzanne. Just finishing my cornflakes. Over.'

'Copy that', Suzanne said, 'Cornflakes. I'm putting my coat on. I'll be out the back. Waiting on the wall. Over and out.'

And I ran and brushed my teeth, and got my bag, and my coat, and Tom.

It's good talking on the walkie-talkies in the mornings. Better than ringing on the doorbell like most people have to. It would be even better if we could take the walkie-talkies to school, but Mum says she doesn't think Mrs Peters would like it, so we have to leave them at home.

When we got to the crossing, me and Suzanne and Tom were the first ones to arrive.

The Lollipop Lady said, 'The early bird catches the worm, eh?'

Tom said, 'I don't like worms.'

'No?' said the Lollipop Lady.

'They wriggle my skin,' Tom said.

'Fair enough,' said the Lollipop Lady. 'Some like carrots and others like cabbage.'

'Come on,' I said, 'we've got to go.'

And the Lollipop Lady said, 'Time is money.' And took us over the road.

Tom loves talking to the Lollipop Lady. Sometimes he talks to her for ages. But we didn't have time to talk to the Lollipop Lady for long that day, because we needed to get into the playground, to wait for Joe, to find out why he had gone to his Dad's and when he was coming home, and what was going to happen to his rabbit and all that.

Me and Suzanne and Tom were the first ones in the playground. After a while other people started coming in; the ones who walk, and the ones on bikes, and the ones from the bus, and Graham Roberts on his Grandad's tractor. Graham Roberts comes to school in all sorts of ways. On his brother's motorbike, and his cousin's combine

277

harvester, and once with his Nan on her electric shopping scooter. But Joe-down-the-road didn't arrive at all. And then the bell went, and everyone went inside.

Mrs Peters said, 'Right, Class Five. Coats on pegs, bags down, bottoms on seats.'

There was a space next to Emma Hendry, where Joe always sits.

When everyone was quiet, Mrs Peters said that she had 'an announcement to make', which means she had something to say. And she said that Joe wasn't coming to school this week, because he was going to go to another school, which was a very nice one, just like ours, in another village, on the other side of the bridge, and he was going to see if he liked it there. And if he *didn't* like it, he was going to come back to our school after Easter, and if he did like it, he was going to stay.

Emma Hendry put her hand up, and Mrs Peters said, 'Yes, Emma?'

And Emma said, 'Can I carry the register when it's Joe's turn?'

And Mrs Peters said, 'No, because if he's not here, Joe won't have a turn, will he?'

And Suzanne said, 'Won't you say Joe's name?'

And Mrs Peters said, 'No.'

And I said, 'What about when Joe comes back?'

And Mrs Peters said, 'If Joe comes back, I will say his name again.'

And then she said, 'Hands up who knows whose will be the last name on the register now?'

And Emma Hendry put her hand up.

'Jake Upton?'

And Jake Upton said, 'Shelly Wainwright is after me.'

And Mrs Peters said, 'That's right. Shelly Wainwright, you will be last on the register.'

And Shelly Wainwright said, 'I don't want to be last. I like being second last.'

And Mrs Peters said, 'Well, that's the way the alphabet works.'

Emma Hendry asked, 'Who is going to sit in Joe's seat next to me if he's not coming back?'

And Suzanne said, 'He probably is coming back, because he's left the New Rabbit behind.'

And I said, 'Yes, because Joe lives down the same road as me and Suzanne.'

Graham Roberts said, 'That's probably why he went away.'

And I said, 'No it isn't.'

And Graham Roberts said, 'Yes it is.'

And I said, 'No it isn't.'

And Graham Roberts said, 'Yes it is.'

And I said, **'NO IT ISN'T!'** And I kicked Graham Roberts under the table. And Graham Roberts kicked me back.

And Mrs Peters said, 'Excuse me! Anna Morris! I am not impressed! Graham Roberts, come and sit next to Emma Hendry, please.'

Emma Hendry did not look very happy that Graham Roberts was going to sit next to her because Graham Roberts swings on his chair, and copies other people's work, and puts their pencils up his nose. And Emma Hendry doesn't like those kinds of things. And also, Graham Roberts always tries to touch Emma Hendry's hair. And then Emma puts her hand up and says, 'Mrs Peters, Graham Roberts is touching my hair again.'

I wouldn't tell Mrs Peters if Graham Roberts touched my hair.

Graham Roberts picked up his things, and went to sit with Emma Hendry. And I wished I hadn't kicked him.

'Who's going to sit next to me?' I said.

'For the time-being, Anna, you can sit by yourself. If you're good this week, I will have another think.'

I undid my trainers and then I did them back up again. And I didn't say anything. Because everyone was looking. And because I didn't want to sit on my own. And because no one can be good for a *week*. And because Joe-down-the-road was moving *schools* as *well* as houses, and no one had told us *that*. And if he still lived at his Mum's house, instead of ages away with his Dad, I wouldn't have to sit on my own, because there wouldn't be a spare seat next to Emma Hendry for Graham Roberts to go and sit in in the first place.

I wrote a note to Suzanne: *'What are we going to do about Joe-down-the-road?'*

Mrs Peters said, 'Anna, writing notes is *not* being good.'

And she took the note off me. And she put it in the bin. And then she did the register. And she stopped at Shelly Wainwright.

After school, Mrs Peters said she had some pictures and work and things that she wanted me and Suzanne to take home to give to Joe next time he came to his Mum's.

Me and Suzanne put all Joe's work up on the walls in the shed. There were paintings and drawings and poems and stories and collages and cut-outs and sums and everything. And they were *all* about his rabbit.

I said, 'How are we going to get Joe-down-the-road back?'

And Suzanne looked at all Joe's work on the walls. 'I don't know,' she said, 'but it's got to be something to do with the New Rabbit.'

⁕ CHAPTER 9 ⁕
Keeping The Rabbit Alive

We didn't know how yet, but me and Suzanne were sure that the New Rabbit was the thing that could make Joe come back and live down the road. And that's why, even though Mum said we had to stay out of it, and stop sticking our noses in, me and Suzanne decided that we'd better start looking after the New Rabbit ourselves. Because if anything bad happened to the New Rabbit, like it died, then Joe would never come back. But while the New Rabbit was here, there was a chance that he might.

Because me and Suzanne heard Joe's Mum talking to my Mum on the phone when we listened in upstairs. And Joe's Mum said Joe didn't really know *where* he wanted to live, or *what* he wanted to do. And the only reason he hadn't taken the New Rabbit with him to his Dad's was because the landlord at Joe's Dad's flat had said, 'No Pets Allowed'.

Suzanne said she bet Joe was worrying about the New Rabbit all the time, now no one was guarding it. Because even though Joe's Mum said Joe would be coming back for Easter, and weekends, and that sort of thing, it still meant the rabbit was hardly ever getting guarded. And, like Joe always said, and like it shows on his pie chart, which we hung up in the shed, 'The more time the rabbit gets guarded, the less chance there is of the rabbit getting got.'

Joe's Mum told my Mum that she was going to

look after the rabbit herself.

When Mum got off the phone, me and Suzanne put the other phone down and went downstairs.

'Who was on the phone?' I asked.

'Joe's Mum.'

'Oh.'

I said, 'Why are no pets allowed at Joe's Dad's flat?'

And Mum said, 'Were you listening in again, Anna?'

I said, 'No.'

And Mum said, 'Mmm.'

I said, 'I don't think Joe's Mum will be very good at looking after Joe's rabbit on her own.'

'I'm sure Pam is quite capable of looking after a rabbit, Anna.'

But me and Suzanne didn't think she was.

Because we had got the binoculars and the notepad out again and done some more spying. And for one thing, Joe's Mum was at work most of the time. And for another thing, she never went in the garden and marched up and down with the Super Soaker. And for an even other thing, she didn't give the rabbit anything to eat. Except millions of dry brown pellets. And you can't just eat those on their own.

Because, like Suzanne said, 'Remember what happened when you tried to eat that pack of crackers?'

Which I had bet Suzanne I could. But in the end I could only eat two because I couldn't even swallow them down. And then a bit went down the wrong way, and I nearly choked to death. And Suzanne had to hit me on the head and throw cold water in my face. And the brown pellets that Joe's Mum gives the New Rabbit are even drier than crackers. Because I tried one.

I said I thought Suzanne was right, and anyway, even if it didn't choke to death, the New Rabbit shouldn't just eat pellets every day because, like Mum says, 'You have to eat fruit and vegetables, Anna, or you will get scurvy and die, like a seventeenth century sailor.'

This is what it says in my dictionary about what scurvy is:

scurvy [skuh-vee] ✦ *noun*
a disease marked by swollen and bleeding gums, livid spots on the skin and suppurating wounds, due to a diet lacking in vitamin C.

And this is what it says in Suzanne's dictionary:

scurvy [skuh-vee] ✦ *noun*
a disease caused by a deficiency of ascorbic acid
characterised by spongy gums, the opening of
previously healed wounds, and bleeding from the
mucous membranes.

And we definitely didn't want Joe's rabbit to get that.

Me and Suzanne decided that as well as making sure it didn't choke to death, or die of scurvy, we'd better start guarding the New Rabbit, in case something else killed it, like the New Cat.

'It isn't just the New Cat that could get the New Rabbit either,' I said, 'because I looked on the computer, and *everything* wants to get rabbits, especially at night. Dogs, and cats, and hawks, and owls, and weasels, and foxes, and farmers, and old ladies who want rabbit's fur for hats.'

And Suzanne said, 'I already knew that.'

And then she said we should make a list of all the things we had to do to make sure the New Rabbit didn't die.

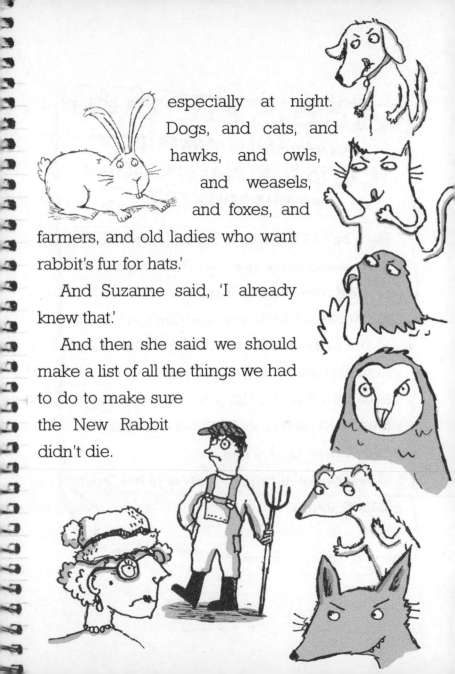

ANNA'S AND SUZANNE'S LIST OF THINGS TO DO TO MAKE SURE THE NEW RABBIT DOESN'T DIE

1. Put a bell on the New Cat's collar so it can't sneak up and scare the New Rabbit to death like it did with the Old Rabbit
2. Put Suzanne's little brother Carl's old baby monitor under the New Rabbit's hutch so we can hear if anything is happening
3. Guard the New Rabbit with Super Soakers
4. Feed the New Rabbit fruit and vegetables so it doesn't get scurvy and die
5. Throw the rabbit's pellets away so it doesn't choke to death

It took quite a long time trying to put the bell on the New Cat's collar. First of all we had to find one. So we went to see Mrs Rotherham, and we told her all about how we needed to put the bell on the New Cat's collar to stop it sneaking up on the New Rabbit and scaring it to death.

Mrs Rotherham said, 'I see. A Cat Attack Alarm. . . I wonder if I can lay my hands on one.' And she went in her cupboard for ages until she did. And then we all had a bowl of ice cream.

And then we had to find the New Cat, and catch it, and then the New Cat attacked us, and then we had to find Tom, to ask him to put the Cat Attack Alarm on the New Cat for us, because he is friends with the New Cat, so it might not mind so much.

And at first Tom said, 'No.'

Because, he said, 'I don't think the New Cat would like to have a Cat Attack Alarm on.'

And Suzanne said, 'We'll give you some biscuits.'

So Tom said, 'Okay.'

And Suzanne pinched some biscuits from her house, and I pinched some from ours, and we gave them to Tom. And Tom put the Cat Attack Alarm on the New Cat's collar. And the New Cat *didn't* want the Cat Attack Alarm on at all. She had a fight with it. But she didn't win because the Cat Attack Alarm stayed on. Tom said he felt sorry for the New Cat. And he sat down, and stroked the New Cat on the head so its ears went flat. And ate all his biscuits.

"CHAPTER 10"
The Tale Of The Fierce Bad Rabbit

The next day after school, while Joe-down-the-road's Mum was still at work, me and Suzanne went to see if Mrs Rotherham had any batteries to put in Carl's old baby monitor.

And we told her all about how we needed it to listen out for Joe's New Rabbit now that Joe wasn't down the road anymore.

Mrs Rotherham said, 'Of course. A Rabbit

Monitor. No rabbit should be without one.'

And she checked inside it and said, 'Mmm... Four double A batteries... I'll see if I can lay my hands on some.'

And after ages in her cupboard, she did. And she put the batteries in the monitor, and she checked it worked by leaving one end of the monitor with us, and taking the other end upstairs and saying, 'Help! Help! It's me, Mrs Rotherham, I'm trapped in the baby monitor. Can anybody hear me?'

And me and Suzanne got The Hysterics. And then we had some ice cream. Because, like Nanna used to say, ice cream is good for calming down.

And then we went down the road and put the listening part of the Rabbit Monitor on the shelf in the shed. And we put the hearing part under the New Rabbit's hutch. And we peered in to have a look at the New Rabbit. There was a lot of hay in the way, all piled up against the wire mesh at the front. Suzanne reached her hand in through the hay and felt around.

'Oh,' she said, 'I can feel it. It's all soft, and fluffy, and warm.'

And then she screamed, **'AGH!'** and she pulled her hand back. Her finger was bleeding. She put it in her mouth.

'It bit me!' she said.

I said, 'Maybe it was asleep, and it got frightened when you put your hand in.' Because when me and Tom had hamsters, our Hamster Manual said that hamsters only bite when they are frightened. And it's probably the same with rabbits.

So I said, 'Things only bite when they're frightened.'

And Suzanne said, 'No, they don't. Some things bite because they like to.'

And I said, 'Like what?'

And Suzanne said, 'Like the New Cat!'

'The New Cat is different,' I said. 'You don't get rabbits like that. Rabbits just hop around, and eat lettuce, and wear yellow ribbons on Easter cards and things.'

Suzanne took her finger out of her mouth. It was still bleeding.

'You put *your* hand in its hutch, then.'

'I will,' I said.

I undid the latch, and

opened the door a crack, and slowly put my hand in the hutch, lying it flat on the bottom, like the Hamster Manual said you should.

I heard something rustle, and then I felt the rabbit's fur against my hand, and its whiskers, and its wet nose.

I kept very still.

'It's sniffing me,' I said. 'It tickles.'

And then I said, '*Nice* New Rabbit.'

And then I said, **'AGH!'**

And pulled my hand away. And put my finger in my mouth. **'It bit me!'**

'*See,*' Suzanne said.

And she put the latch back on.

The New Rabbit rustled in the hay. It pushed its way through to the front of the hutch. It was white. And it had pink eyes. And it was Absolutely

Enormous. The New Rabbit stared out at us through the wire mesh.

Suzanne said, 'Look at its eyes!'

And I said, 'Look at its ears!'

And Suzanne said, 'Look at its teeth!'

And I said, 'Look at its claws!'

And Suzanne said, 'When did it get so *big?*'

Because the last time me and Suzanne had seen the New Rabbit, it was tiny. And its eyes were closed. And it fitted inside Joe's hand.

The New Rabbit gnawed on the wire on the front of the hutch. It had long yellow teeth.

Suzanne said, 'It's not like Joe's *Old* Rabbit, is it?'

And it wasn't, because if you put your hand in the Old Rabbit's hutch, the Old Rabbit would rub its head against you, and hop onto your hand to be taken out. And then, if you let it, it would go up your jumper and nuzzle your neck.

You couldn't fit the New Rabbit up your jumper. Not even if you wanted to. And you wouldn't want to anyway.

We stared at the New Rabbit. And the New Rabbit stared back at us.

Suzanne said, 'It's too big for the hutch.'

Which was true. It was almost as big as the hutch itself.

'Maybe that's why it looks angry,' I said.

Because the Old Rabbit had lots of room to hop around. But if the New Rabbit stretched out, its feet would touch both ends of the hutch.

301

I said, 'We could let it out for a bit.'

And Suzanne said, 'How will we get it back in?'

'We won't let it *out* out,' I said. 'We'll just let it out in the run. For a few minutes. And then we'll shoo it back in.'

And Suzanne said, 'Good idea.'

Which Suzanne hardly ever says, so that meant it was.

We picked up the run from the corner of the garden and put it on the front of the hutch. And it fitted just right. Because that's how Joe's Dad had made it, ages ago, for the Old Rabbit, when he still lived with Joe and Joe's Mum.

There was a small hole in the wire mesh, in one corner of the run. We looked at the hole, and we looked at the rabbit. The hole was about the size of a jam jar. And the rabbit was about the size of a dog. In fact, it was bigger than a dog. It was bigger than Miss Matheson's dog anyway, because that's only the same size as a guinea pig.

'The rabbit can't fit through the hole,' I said.

'No, definitely not,' said Suzanne.

← Rabbit

←Hole

So we opened the door of the hutch. And the rabbit hopped out into the run. And it stood very still in the middle of the run, and it sniffed the air, and it put its ears right up. And then it hopped over to the corner with the hole. And it looked at the hole. And then, in a second, it squeezed through it.

Suzanne said, **'IT'S OUT!'**

And I said, 'The gate!'

I ran to the gate and slammed it shut. The rabbit looked angrier than ever. It thumped its back leg on the ground. I tried to grab the rabbit. And Suzanne tried to grab the rabbit. But whenever we got near it, the New Rabbit ran at us and scrabbled and scratched and tried to bite.

I said, 'We need gardening gloves.' Like Mum uses to put the New Cat in its carry case to take it to the vet's.

And I ran up the road to the shed to get them.

When I got back, Suzanne was running round Joe's garden in circles, and the New Rabbit was running after her.

'*Suzanne,*' I said. 'Turn around and run *at* the rabbit, to shoo it towards me. I'll get it with the gardening gloves.'

And she did.

I grabbed hold of the rabbit. It scrabbled and scratched and clawed and kicked. But I held onto it, tight.

And then I felt it bite. The blood came right through the gardening gloves. I dropped the rabbit. And ran up the road with my finger in my mouth.

I got a plaster from the house for my hand. And I went into the shed and got my big brother Andy's cricket pads and his cycle helmet. I put them on. And I put his gum shield in my mouth. I took his shin pads, some old oven gloves and a balaclava for Suzanne. And I got two fishing nets.

When I got back, Suzanne was in the corner of Joe's garden, pressed against the fence, and the New Rabbit was in front of her, and it was making a growling sound. There were scratches all over Suzanne's legs.

I said, 'I didn't know rabbits growled.'

And Suzanne said, **'HELP!'**

'You need to get to the gate!'

'I can't! I'm stuck.'

'Jump!' I said.

Suzanne jumped right over the rabbit, and ran for the gate. And when she got through it, she slammed it shut. I gave Suzanne the shin pads, and the oven gloves, and the gum shield and the balaclava.

And she put them on.

Then we got The Hysterics because we looked quite funny, and we had to lie down on the pavement for a bit.

And then we stopped having The Hysterics, because it wasn't funny really, because, like Suzanne said, 'This is *serious*.'

So we went back in.

The rabbit stood still in the middle of the grass, sniffing the air, with its enormous ears up. We took a step towards it, and it thumped its back leg on the ground, and growled again.

'Ready?' I said.

And Suzanne said, 'Yes.'

We ran at the New Rabbit,

and we tried to catch it under the fishing nets, but the New Rabbit was too quick. And the fishing nets were too small. And it hopped and jumped and ran all around the garden, and the more we chased it, the further away it got.

And then, suddenly, the New Rabbit stopped, and it got up on its hind legs, and it put its ears right up, and it sniffed the air. And it stared at the gate. And it froze.

The gate started to open. And I thought me and Suzanne were in Big Trouble then, because it was probably Joe's Mum.

But it wasn't, it was Tom. And he wasn't on his own. He was with the New Cat.

When it saw the New Rabbit, the New Cat's eyes went very wide, and it got down very low.

And it stared at the New Rabbit. And the New Rabbit got down low too, and stared back at the New Cat. And they stayed very still.

And the rabbit went, '**GGRRRRRRRR.**'

And the cat went, '*Ttsssss.*'

And then the New Rabbit turned, and shot back through the hole in the run, and up into its hutch. And Suzanne closed the door, and I fastened the latch.

When I got home, Mum said, 'Anna, where did you get all those scratches?'

And I said, 'From Suzanne.'

CHAPTER 11
Rabbit Food

After that, even though me and Suzanne decided we didn't really like the New Rabbit, we started looking after it all the time. We sat on the pavement outside Joe's house with Super Soakers, and we took turns to take the Rabbit Monitor to bed at night. We fed the New Rabbit every morning on the way to school, and every afternoon on the way back. And at first we put in things we found at home, but then Mum said, 'I could have sworn I had some spinach.'

And, 'Has anyone seen the celery?'

And, 'How can you *lose* a *leek*?'

And when Suzanne's Dad said,

'WHAT ON **EARTH** HAS HAPPENED TO ALL MY HERBS?', we started getting things from other places instead.

We got apples from Mr Tucker's tree, and cress from the window ledge in the classroom at school, and privet leaves from Miss Matheson's hedge.

And we wanted to get the parsley from Miss Matheson's back garden too. But Miss Matheson kept spotting us and tapping on her window, saying, **'Private property! Private property! I won't have my plants purloined!'**

And then she phoned Mum to complain.

This is what it says in my dictionary about purloining…

purloin [pur-loyn] ✦ *noun*
to take dishonestly; filch; pilfer

This is what it said in Suzanne's dictionary…

purloin [pur-loyn] ✦ *noun*
steal

Suzanne didn't used to have her own dictionary. She used to borrow her Dad's. But the last time Suzanne took it, it went in the toilet by mistake, and Suzanne's Dad said, **'FOR CRYING OUT LOUD, IT'S COMPLETELY RUINED, SUZANNE!'** And he threw it in the bin.

He bought a new dictionary, and he said,

'IF YOU GO **ANYWHERE** NEAR IT, SUZANNE, YOUR LIFE WILL **NOT BE WORTH LIVING!**'

But Suzanne didn't need to go anywhere near it anyway because we got the old dictionary out of the bin and dried it out in our airing cupboard, and stuck the pages that had torn back together, and now it's as good as before, except the pages are a bit wobbly and it smells a bit strange.

Anyway, when me and Suzanne first started feeding the New Rabbit, we had to be quick getting our hands in and out of the hutch, because as soon as we opened the latch, the New Rabbit attacked us.

313

But on the second day it didn't bite, and on the third day it let us stroke it. And at first we thought it was because the New Rabbit was starting to like us. But on the fourth day, when the New Rabbit didn't even get up, and hardly opened its eyes, Suzanne said, 'I don't think the New Rabbit is very well.'

And I said that I didn't think it was either. Because its fur looked funny, and it had red patches all over its chest.

When we told Tom all about how the New Rabbit was sick, Tom said, 'When Peter Rabbit is poorly, Mrs Rabbit gives him camomile tea.'

Me and Suzanne looked in the cupboards in Suzanne's kitchen, and then we looked in the cupboards in my kitchen, but we couldn't find any camomile tea. We did find some other tea

though, which it said on the
box was 'made only with
the finest tips'. Which we
thought would be just as
good.

I'm not supposed to
make hot drinks because,
once, I tried to make coffee, and
I forgot to put water in the kettle, and I put half a jar
of coffee granules in instead, and when I turned it
on, the kettle made a fizzing noise and went **BANG!**
And that's why there's a big black patch on the
kitchen counter.

So we made the tea very quickly, and went
outside and waited for it to cool down, and then
we took it down the road and we tipped the New
Rabbit's water out of its bowl and we poured the

tea in instead. Then we went back to the shed.

And after a while Mum came and she knocked on the door and she said, 'Have you been using the kettle again and trying to make tea in the kitchen?'

And I said, 'No.'

And Mum said, 'Mmm.'

And then she said, 'What are you two *up* to?'

And Suzanne said, 'Nothing.'

And Mum said, 'Mmm.'

And then she said that Joe-down-the-road was coming home tomorrow, after school, for Easter, and that me and Suzanne should call on him and try to be kind, and that we should do the things Joe wanted, even if it was boring, like guarding his rabbit.

CHAPTER 12

Joe's Down The Road Again

In the morning, when Joe's Dad's van pulled into the road, me and Suzanne were standing at Joe's gate with our Super Soakers.

Joe and his Dad got out. Joe's Dad said, 'Armed guard, eh, girls?'

And we said, 'Yes.'

'Can't be too careful,' he said, and he held up his hands, and we let him pass, and he went inside. And me and Suzanne told Joe all about how we had been guarding the New Rabbit, in secret, and how we had put the Cat Attack Alarm on the New Cat's collar so it couldn't sneak up and scare the New Rabbit to death, and we showed him the Rabbit Monitor, under the hutch, and told him how the other end was in the shed, and how at night we took turns taking it to bed so we would hear if anything happened.

But we didn't tell him about how we had let the New Rabbit out by mistake, or how the New Cat had seen it, or how Joe's Mum was only giving it bowls of brown pellets, and how we had to feed it ourselves, because like Mum said to us before we left the house, 'Don't go worrying Joe about his rabbit.'

Joe looked in at the New Rabbit, and he opened the hutch, and he put his hand in and pushed back some of the straw.

'I don't think the New Rabbit is very well.'

he said. 'Normally, the New Rabbit bites.'

'Oh,' I said.

'Does it?' said Suzanne.

And we pulled our sleeves over our hands to cover our scratches and plasters.

Joe looked in the hutch again. He said that the New Rabbit's poos were all wrong, because they're supposed to be small and hard, not wet and stuck to its bum. Then he looked at the New Rabbit's chest. And he said its fur had gone strange, and it didn't normally have red patches like that.

And then Joe's Dad came out of the house. And he mended the hole in the wire in the rabbit run. And he went to the van, and he got a paper bag out, and he gave it to Joe.

And he said, 'I've told your Mum about the medicine. Don't forget to take it, champ.'

And Joe said, 'No.'

Joe's Dad gave him a cuddle. And he scrubbed him on the head. And he got in the van and drove away.

Joe watched the van go.

'What medicine?' said Suzanne.

Joe showed her. There was a tube of cream, and a bottle of liquid. The tube said 'Florasone' and the bottle said 'Imodium'.

Suzanne looked at the bottle, and at the tube.

And then she looked at the rabbit. And then she looked at Joe.

And then she said, 'You and the rabbit are *both* poorly.'

And Joe said, 'Yes.'

And then Joe's Mum came out. And she kissed Joe all over his face until Joe went red. And then she said, 'Sorry, Joe.' And then she kissed again.

Joe told his Mum that he thought the New Rabbit was poorly.

And Joe's Mum said that she knew, and that she was keeping a close eye on the rabbit, and she checked the New Rabbit's chest, and she looked in its mouth and she said, 'He hasn't been himself. I've spoken to the vet and if he's not any better tomorrow, we'll take him to see her.'

And then she lifted up Joe's t-shirt, and she looked at *his* chest too, and it had a red rash all over it, and she looked in his mouth. And she said, 'And if *you* aren't any better tomorrow, we'll take you to the vet's as well.'

And she kissed Joe again. And then she said that her and Joe were going to have some lunch.

And me and Suzanne said that if Joe wanted, he could come up to the shed after, and we would let him be in our clubs.

On the way up the road, Suzanne said, 'Let's go on the computer and look something up.' Which Suzanne never normally wants to do.

We sat down at the screen and Suzanne put in 'Florasone', and it said, '`Florasone: a cream for eczema.`'

And then she put in 'Imodium' and it said, '**Imodium: for upset stomachs and diarrhoea.**'

And then she put in 'diarrhoea and eczema' and she said, 'Let's print these pages off.'

I went and asked Mum. I'm not allowed to print things without asking anymore after I printed off two hundred and forty three pages for Tom about Batman and Bob the Builder.

Mum came with the printer cable and she looked at the screen and she said, 'Why do you want to print off descriptions of eczema and diarrhoea?'

'It's for Suzanne,' I said.

Suzanne scratched her chest and rubbed her stomach. 'I'm not well,' she said.

Mum said, 'Mmm' and pressed 'Print'.

Suzanne put the pages in her pocket.

And Mum made us some cheese sandwiches and some squash and we took them out to the shed, and we ate our sandwiches and read what it said about eczema and diarrhoea.

Suzanne said, 'Joe and the New Rabbit have got exactly the same things wrong with them.'

'Have they?'

'Yes. At exactly the same time.'

'Oh.'

'Both of them were fine before Joe went away.'

'So?' I said.

And Suzanne said, *'So. . .'*

I asked Suzanne if she wanted the rest of her sandwich.

And Suzanne said, 'No.'

So I had it instead. And I said, 'It's probably a coincidence.'

'It *could* be a coincidence,' Suzanne said. 'But it could be *connected*.'

'Why?'

'Because,' Suzanne said, 'Joe and the New Rabbit were both fine. And then Joe and the New Rabbit got separated. And that's when Joe and the New Rabbit got poorly. So now Joe and the New Rabbit are back together again, what's going to happen?'

'I don't know,' I said. Because I hate riddles and things like that because I never know the answer.

'They might both get better again. And if they do, it can't just be a coincidence, can it?

325

It has to be connected.'

And I said, 'I don't know.' Because I didn't.

This is what it says a 'coincidence' is in my dictionary:

coincidence [co-in-si-dense] ✦ *noun*
a striking occurrence of two or more events
at one time, apparently by mere chance or
accident

This it what it says 'connected' is in
my dictionary:

connected [con-ec-ted] ✦ *noun*
to be joined together or linked

I didn't know if Joe and the New Rabbit being poorly with the same thing at the same time was a coincidence, or if it was connected, but I was glad we didn't have to look after the New Rabbit for two weeks while Joe was back down the road for Easter.

Because it's quite hard work, looking after a rabbit. Especially when you aren't supposed to be looking after it, and you have to do it in secret, and hide behind the hedge to guard it, and steal all its food for it, and listen to it on the Rabbit Monitor in bed every other night.

Now Joe was back to look after his rabbit himself, me and Suzanne could do all the other things that we used to do before we had to look after the New Rabbit all the time.

So I said, 'Let's do something.'

327

And Suzanne said, 'What?'

'I don't know.'

We sat on the roof and tried to think.

And Suzanne said she wondered what Joe was doing now. And whether he had finished his lunch.

And I said so did I.

And Suzanne said she wondered if Joe would come up to the shed.

And I said that he probably wouldn't, because he would probably just go back to guarding his rabbit all the time.

And then we saw Joe coming up the back lane.

And we got down from the roof, and we told Joe the password, and we let him in the shed, and we showed him how we had put all his work up on the walls, and how we had the Rabbit Monitor

328

on the shelf to listen out for the New Rabbit. And Joe looked pretty pleased.

'Shall we play Dingo The Dog?' I said.

At first Joe didn't want to, but Suzanne gave him the Rabbit Monitor to put in his pocket so he could hear if anything happened. And then he said, 'okay.'

And Suzanne went and got Barney's old collar and lead, and we went out the back and played Dingo the Dog.

And afterwards we went to Joe's house, and we played Mountain Rescue. And Joe's Mum got us fish and chips. And she said me and Suzanne could stay the night, if we liked. And we did.

So we went home to get our pyjamas and toothbrushes and all that.

And Suzanne told Joe about how it isn't as good in Mrs Peters' class without him. And how Shelly Wainwright is last on the register, and how she doesn't like being last because she liked being second last, like she was when Joe was there.

And I told Joe about how Mrs Peters made Graham Roberts move, and sit in Joe's seat, and how I had to sit on my own, and I didn't like it. And I said that it was probably much better at Joe's new school.

But Joe said it wasn't, because he liked Mrs Peters because she didn't mind him not putting his hand up, and doing all his work about rabbits and everything, but his new teacher did mind.

And everyone called him Joseph instead of Joe.

And Suzanne said, 'Mrs Peters said you could come back to our school after Easter if you didn't like it at your new one.'

And Joe said, 'I can't, because after Mum shouted at me about always guarding the New Rabbit, I shouted back and said, **'I WANT TO LIVE WITH DAD!'** And Mum said that I could if I really wanted to. And I said I did. And I phoned Dad and he said that he would come and get me in the morning the morning came I didn't want to go, but I had to then because that's what I'd said. And I didn't want Dad to think I didn't want to live with him.' Which is like when I went to live with Mrs Rotherham. When I didn't really want to. Before Tom came to rescue me.

And then Joe showed us a list that he had done
and it said:

GOOD **THINGS** ABOUT LIVING
WITH MY DAD:

I see my Dad every day

BAD **THINGS** ABOUT LIVING WITH MY DAD:

The New Rabbit isn't there

The food

My bed

There's no one to play with

Dad's New Girlfriend

I don't like the school

Mum isn't there

And then Joe drew us a picture of his Dad's flat, and where his bedroom is at the back, and how you get there.

You go down our road and past the horse trough, and the shops, and the Bottom Bus Stop, and over the bridge and round the roundabout, and down the lane, and through the gate, and over the stile, and through the old tunnel and down the track, and then you're there.

And Joe said that maybe me and Suzanne could come and see him soon, after school.

And Suzanne said that we probably couldn't, because it was way past the Bottom Bus Stop and everything, which is Out Of Bounds.

And Joe said, 'You could come on the Super-Speed-Bike-Machine, and bring me back on the stunt pegs.'

333

And I said how we weren't allowed to get the Super-Speed-Bike-Machine out anymore after we went into the road and Tom hit his head and had to have six sticky stitches.

And Joe said, 'Oh.'

And then he wrote, 'Map to Joe's Dad's flat' on the top of the paper. And he said we could have it anyway, just in case.

And I said we would pin it on the wall in the shed. And we would go when we were old enough.

And Joe said I should put the list of things he didn't like about living with his Dad in the shed as well, because he didn't want his Dad to see it.

So I folded the list and the map up, and I put them in my bag.

And then Suzanne started making funny noises and opening and closing her mouth. And snoring. And I held her nose, and me and Joe got The Hysterics.

And Suzanne woke up and said it wasn't funny actually because she couldn't help it and she might have to have her adenoids out.

This is what it says about adenoids in my dictionary:

adenoids [ad-en-oyd-s] ✦ *noun*
the soft mass of flesh between the back of the nose and the throat, which sometimes makes breathing difficult

In the morning, me and Suzanne and Joe-down-the-road played Mountain Rescue again, and Dingo the Dog, and Tom played too. And we sat on the shed roof and did other things, like seeing how long we could stare at the sun before we went blind, and how long we could hold our breath before we died, and talking about the Super-Speed-Bike-Machine.

And after that, as soon as he had finished his breakfast, and looked after his rabbit, Joe came up the road to meet me and Suzanne every day.

And every day Suzanne said, 'How's the New Rabbit?'

And every day Joe said, 'Better.'

And then Suzanne said, 'And how are *you*?'

And Joe looked at her a bit funny, because it's

not like Suzanne is always asking people how they are or anything.

And he said, 'I'm better too.'

And Suzanne kept looking at Joe's chest, and asking him about his poo. And looking in on the New Rabbit and checking its poos and its chest too. And when Joe wasn't looking she wrote it all down in the Spy Club notebook: 10.00 am, Tuesday. Joe much better. Rabbit much better too.

And she said to me, 'Joe and the rabbit are getting better every day.'

And I said, 'So?'

And Suzanne said, 'They were both fine, and then when Joe went away, they both got poorly. And now Joe is back, they are both fine again.'

And then she said, 'It *can't* just be a coincidence.'

CHAPTER 13

Purloining Miss Matheson's Parsley

The day Joe gave us the Rabbit Monitor back and left to go to his Dad's, me and Suzanne promised him we would keep looking after the New Rabbit.

So, that afternoon, we collected privet leaves and daffodils. And then we got the binoculars and the Spy Club notebook out of the shed and we started to spy on Miss Matheson because, even though we're banned, we had to get some of her parsley for the New Rabbit in case it got poorly again, because, like Tom said, 'Before the camomile tea, Peter Rabbit eats some parsley to make him feel better.'

We looked over Miss Matheson's fence with the binoculars.

And Suzanne wrote down in the notebook:

2:45pm – Miss Matheson digging her parsley up

3:15 pm – Miss Matheson putting parsley on her compost heap.

3:30 pm – Miss Matheson going into her house

We sneaked in over the gate, and we ran to the compost heap and took as much of the parsley as we could carry, and we put it in the shed. The parsley that grows in Miss Matheson's garden is just like normal parsley, except much taller, and fatter, and it smells strange. And then we shut the shed, and locked the padlock, and we went down the road with the privet leaves and the daffodils and a little piece of parsley.

The New Rabbit was back to how it used to be, before Joe left, and it tried to bite us when we put our hands in.

We sat and watched it eat the privet and the daffodils. And we gave it the little bit of parsley, just to make sure.

And I said, 'Maybe the New Rabbit is going to be fine.'

And Suzanne said, 'Maybe.'

ꞏ CHAPTER 14 ꞏ
'Til Death Do Us Part

In the morning it was the first day back at school, and me and Suzanne and Tom looked in on the New Rabbit on the way, and gave it some more of the parsley to eat, but the rabbit didn't try to bite. It was just lying still again.

Suzanne said, 'The rabbit was fine, and then Joe went away and the rabbit was poorly. And then Joe came back, and the rabbit got better. And now Joe has gone away again, and the rabbit is poorly again. It *can't* be a coincidence.'

And I said, 'It *has* to be connected.'

We must have fed the rabbit for too long because Suzanne looked at her watch and jumped up and said, 'It's five to nine!'

I haven't got a watch because I lost mine, and anyway, like Suzanne says, even when I did have one it didn't help because I'm not very good at telling the time.

We closed the hutch and fastened the latch and ran as fast as we could, and at first we thought the Lollipop Lady had gone home because she wasn't standing at the crossing. But when we got closer we saw she was sitting on the bench, under the conker tree, reading a paper.

The Lollipop Lady stood up, and a gust of wind whipped her newspaper out of her hands, and the pages went everywhere and she ran around trying to grab them.

'Well, if it's not one thing, it's another,' she said.

And me and Suzanne and Tom ran around as well, picking up the pages, and we gave them all back, except I saw Suzanne take one page and fold it up and put it in her pocket.

And Suzanne said, 'We're late.'

And the Lollipop Lady said, 'Shake a leg, then.'

And she took us over the road.

And we shouted, **'THANKS'** and went over the wall, and into the playground.

And the Lollipop Lady shouted after us, 'BETTER LATE THAN NEVER. BLAME IT ON THE RAIN!' Even though it wasn't raining.

Tom ran to his classroom and me and Suzanne ran to ours.

And Miss Peters looked at the clock and said, 'What time do you call this?'

And I didn't know what time to call it because I can only do the o'clocks and the half pasts and it wasn't one of those.

And Suzanne said she called it, 'Quarter past nine.'

And then she said, 'The Lollipop Lady's newspaper blew away, and we had to help her catch it.'

And Mrs Peters said, 'Mmm.'

And then she said, 'Sit down.'

At play-time, me and Suzanne went up into the

top corner of the field, and Suzanne showed me the piece of newspaper that she had folded up and put in her pocket. It said:

WOMAN'S SHED NEARLY BURNS DOWN.

'Not that bit,' said Suzanne, 'look!' And she pointed to the part underneath. It said:

CAN'T LIVE APART

Local couple Sidney and Edith Armstrong both died last week within hours of each other, having been separated into different care homes. A friend said, 'Sidney and Edith were fine before. Doctors can say what they like, but I know that they died of broken hearts.'

I read it twice. And I said, 'It's just like Joe and the New Rabbit.'

On the way home from school, me and Suzanne and Tom went to get some of Miss Matheson's tall parsley from the shed. The smell wafted out when we opened the door.

We took a piece down to the New Rabbit. It looked even worse than ever.

Suzanne said, 'What if the New Rabbit dies?' We went back to the shed.

Suzanne got the newspaper page out of her pocket and pinned it on the wall next to the map to Joe's Dad's flat, and the list of things Joe didn't like about living at his Dad's.

'What are we going to do?' I asked.

Suzanne said, 'We have to get Joe and his rabbit back together.'

We started making a plan.

ANNA'S AND TOM'S AND SUZANNE'S PLANS TO GET JOE-DOWN-THE-ROAD AND THE NEW RABBIT BACK TOGETHER AND RESCUE THEM BEFORE THEY BOTH DIE

PLAN NUMBER 1

Tell Mum that Joe and his rabbit are going to die and ask her to go and rescue Joe

PLAN NUMBER 2

Get Joe's Dad's phone number and phone Joe and tell him that his rabbit and him are going to die if he doesn't come home

PLAN NUMBER 3

Write Joe's Dad a letter pretending to be the landlord and tell him that the rules have changed from 'NO PETS' to 'NO PETS EXCEPT RABBITS'

PLAN NUMBER 4

Go and rescue Joe ourselves

There was a knock on the shed door.

'What's the password?' I said.

Mum said, 'Trouble. Your tea is ready. And Suzanne's Dad's been on the phone.'

So we pinned the plan on the wall, and Suzanne took the Rabbit Monitor because it was her turn, and we came out of the shed, and I locked the padlock.

And Mum said, 'What is that awful smell?'

And Suzanne said, 'Tom.' Even though it was really Miss Matheson's parsley.

And Mum said, 'Tom, that's a big smell for a small person. Maybe you should go to the toilet.'

And me and Tom went inside. And Suzanne went home. And we heard Suzanne's Dad shouting through the wall about what time it was, and where she'd been, and coming straight home from school and all that.

After tea, when Mum was watching 'Coronation Street', I said, 'Mum...'

And Mum said, 'Yes...'

'Can you drive to Joe-down-the-road's Dad's

flat and rescue Joe, please?'

And Mum said, 'Mmm?'

And then she said, 'No.'

And Tom said, 'Why?'

'Because it's a school night.'

And I said, 'Please.'

And Mum said, 'No.'

And Tom said, 'Why?'

'Because.'

And Tom said, 'If you don't, Joe's New Rabbit and Joe will die.'

And Mum said, 'Joe's Rabbit is fine. And so is Joe. No one needs to be rescued!'

And I said, 'What's Joe's Dad's phone number?'

And Mum said, 'Why?'

And I said, 'Because.'

And Mum said, 'Are you going to tell Joe this

rubbish about his rabbit dying?'

'No.'

Mum gave me Joe's number. I
dialled it. Mum was still standing in the room,
so I said, 'Did you want something?' Because
that's what Mum always says to me when I hang
around when *she's* on the phone.

Mum said, '*Watch* it, Anna.' And went away.

Joe's Dad answered.

'Is Joe there?'

And he put Joe on.

'Hello, Joe.'

I heard Mum pick up the other phone upstairs.
Mum doesn't know that you have to hold the
'quiet' button down if you don't want the other
person to know you're listening in.

So I couldn't say anything about the New Rabbit

and how me and Suzanne had found out that Joe and the New Rabbit were probably going to die.

So I just said, 'Can you tell me your address, please, because me and Suzanne want to send you a birthday card.'

And Joe said, 'It isn't my birthday until August.'

And I said, 'So?'

'That's in four months.'

I said, 'We have to make it first.'

'Oh.'

Joe told me the address and I wrote it down.

And then he said, 'Is the New Rabbit okay?'

And I was going to say, 'No', but I heard Mum

say, 'Eh hem' on the other phone, so I said, 'Yes. It's fine.'

And then I said, 'How are *you?*'

And Joe said, 'Itchy. My eczema's back.'

And I said, 'Okay, then. Bye.' And I put the phone down.

Mum came down and said, 'Why do you want Joe's address?'

And I said, 'Were you listening in?' Because that's what Mum always says to me.

And Mum said, '*Anna…*'

And I said, 'I'm going to see Suzanne.'

And Mum said, 'No. You're not. You going to do your homework, and read your book and then it's time for bed.'

I went into my bedroom and I got the walkie-talkie, 'Anna to Suzanne. Anna to Suzanne. Come in, Suzanne. Over.'

'Suzanne to Anna. Suzanne to Anna. Receiving you loud and clear. Over.'

'I have tried Plan One.' (Which was the one about getting Mum to drive to Joe's house to rescue him.) 'But Mum says she won't rescue Joe. And I have tried to do Plan Two.' (Which is the one where we phone Joe to tell him to come home.) 'But I couldn't talk to Joe about it because Mum was listening in and she said I wasn't allowed to say anything to Joe about his rabbit. Over.'

'Copy that. We will have to try Plan Three. Over.'

Which was the one where we write a letter to Joe's Dad from the landlord.

I was going to tell Suzanne about how Joe had

said that his eczema had come back again, but I didn't get a chance to say anything else because Mum came in and she took the walkie-talkie off me and she said, 'Homework!'

And I heard Suzanne saying, 'Anna? Anna? Are you receiving me? Over.'

°CHAPTER 15 °
'Rabbits Don't Scream'

In the morning we went and looked in on the New Rabbit again and took it some more of the tall smelly parsley from the shed. The rabbit looked even worse than before. On the way to school, Suzanne said that she had had a dream in the night and in her dream the rabbit was screaming.

I said, 'I don't think rabbits scream.'

And Suzanne said, 'In my dream it did.'

After school, Suzanne brought all her pens to the shed. We decided that Suzanne should write the letter because she has got the best handwriting. And I said what she should write down. We had to do a lot of practice letters, because for one thing Suzanne isn't very good at spelling and she kept putting the words all wrong. And for another thing, I kept changing my mind about what the words should be, like whether it should say 'from' or 'love from' or 'yours sincerely'.

Anyway, in the end we put…

Dear Mr Walker (Joe's Dad),

I have changed the rules about pets from NO PETS to NO PETS EXCEPT RABBITS. If you see me do not ask me about rabbits though, please, because I don't want to talk about it.

Yours sincerely,

The Landlord

P.S. Please do not let the rabbit go on the stairs or in the lift because I do not want poos and rabbit fluff getting trodden into the carpet.

We put the letter in an envelope, and Suzanne wrote the address on it, and I put a stamp on, and licked the envelope shut, and we took it to the post box at the bottom of the road, and we lifted Tom up to post it, because posting letters is one of Tom's best things.

And Suzanne said she couldn't stop thinking about her dream with the rabbit screaming.

So we went home, and we put 'rabbit screaming' in the computer and this is what it said…

'A rabbit scream is a shrill sound, not unlike the scream of a small child. It generally signifies the rabbit is dying.'

CHAPTER 16
A Real-Life Rescue

I was in bed when I heard it. It woke me up.

Mum came into my room. 'Anna, what's the matter?' She felt me on the forehead. 'You screamed,' she said, 'did you have a bad dream?'

I said that I had.

Mum stroked me on the head. And I lay back down and pretended to fall asleep until she went back to bed.

Because it wasn't *me* who had screamed. It had come from under my bed. Where the Rabbit Monitor was.

I got my walkie-talkie and I whispered, 'Suzanne, are you asleep?'

Suzanne didn't speak.

'Suzanne, are you there?' I went under the covers. *'SUZANNE, THE RABBIT SCREAMED!'*

The walkie-talkie crackled. 'Copy that,' Suzanne said. 'Meet me at the shed. Over and out.'

I got out of bed and felt my way, in the dark, through my bedroom door and along the wall in the corridor, until I came to the top of the stairs. I'm not scared of the dark, because I'm nine, but some things in our house aren't nice at night, when the lights aren't on. Like the photo of Dad's Great-Grandma with the black lace veil on her face, and the spider-plant with the tentacles that touch you when you go past, and the post with the coats on, at the bottom of the

360

stairs, that sometimes looks like a person.

And this time, the stair-post looked *a lot* like a person. And as I got near it, I saw one of the arms was reaching out. And when I got to the bottom, I thought it tried to touch me.

I ran past it, into the kitchen, to the back door, and turned the handle fast. And then I felt something behind me, tapping me on the back. I froze.

'Are you going out?'

'Tom?!'

'Yes?'

'Oh.' I turned around. He was in his Batman pyjamas, and his Bob the Builder hard hat.

'I thought you were something else.'

'No,' Tom said. 'Where are you going?'

'To the shed.'

'I'll come.'

And I said that he could because, for one thing, he was already putting his wellies on and, for another thing, I didn't want him getting the Screaming Habdabs and waking up Mum and, for an even other thing, I was glad it was him who had tapped me on the back, and not a coat that had got down off the stair-post, on its own, or anything like that.

It was cold outside, and the moon was out, and the stars. The sky was big. And when I looked up, it made me feel a bit sick. It was quiet. I held my nose and popped my ears, to hear clearer.

Tom turned the torch on, on his Bob the Builder hard hat. The light shone on Suzanne. She was waiting by the shed.

'Follow me,' she said.

The back lane looked different in the dark.

'Come on, Tom,' I said, and I told him it was best to look straight ahead, not out to the sides, where the bushes are, because in the dark you can sometimes see things that aren't really there. And I said that if he wanted, he could hold onto my hand. But Tom said he was Batman, and Bob the Builder, so he wasn't scared.

When we got to the bottom, I looked up at Joe's house. It was so dark you couldn't see the windows, or the door, only the shape of the outside. Like the houses Mrs Peters cut out of black card, to put at the back of the stage, when we did the school play.

Suzanne opened the gate.

We crouched down by the hutch. I opened the latch, and pushed back some of the hay. The New Rabbit was on its side. There was dribble round its mouth. And its eyes were all strange.

'Is it dead?' Tom said.

The New Rabbit groaned, and twitched its feet.

'Not yet,' said Suzanne.

'What are we going to do?' I asked.

Suzanne said we should go back to the shed and make a plan.

I was glad to get away from the New Rabbit, and to be inside the shed with the worms and the woodlice and the wasp trap and all that. I closed the door. We looked at the plans, pinned up on the wall.

'We've tried Plan Number One, and Number Two, and Number Three,' Suzanne said.

There was only one plan left. It was Plan Number Four: Rescue Joe Ourselves. I looked at the map to his Dad's flat, that Joe had drawn. It was a long way away. Past the Bottom Bus Stop, and over the bridge, and round the roundabout, and down the track, and through the old tunnel, and across the field. All in the dark.

'Joe's Dad might come and collect the New Rabbit in the morning, when he reads our letter from the landlord,' I said. 'And if he doesn't, we could rescue Joe tomorrow, straight after school.'

'Tomorrow might be too late,' Suzanne said. 'We need to go tonight.'

'How are we going to get there?' I asked.

'We'll walk,' said Suzanne.

I said I didn't think walking was a good idea.

'How else?' Suzanne said.

'Erm... bus?'

Suzanne made her eyebrows go up, and said, '*Anna,*' the way I hate. 'You don't get buses in the middle of the *night.*'

And I said how you did, actually, and that's why it's called a night bus.

Suzanne said she had never heard of a night bus, and there was, 'no such thing.'

And I said that just because she didn't know about it, didn't mean it didn't exist. Because there were millions of things in the world that Suzanne had never heard of. And I tried to think of one, which was hard because Suzanne has actually heard of most things, and because Tom kept pulling at my pyjamas and saying, 'Anna… Anna… ANNA…'

So I stopped trying to think, and said, **'WHAT?!'**

'Look.' Tom was pointing to something shiny, at the back of the shed, near the floor, underneath an old sheet. The light from his Bob the Builder hard hat was making it glint.

I went closer. It was a reflector, on the spoke of a bicycle wheel. I pulled away the old sheet. *'The Super-Speed-Bike-Machine!'*

Me and Suzanne checked the stabilisers, and the tyres, and the lights. And Tom rang the bell, and made the wheels spin round, and all the reflectors shone, and the spokies went up and down.

And Suzanne said we should write a list of things we needed.

So we did. This is what it said...

ANNA'S AND SUZANNE'S AND TOM'S LIST
OF THINGS WE NEED TO RESCUE
JOE-DOWN-THE-ROAD

The Super-Speed-Bike-Machine

Tom's Bob the Builder hard hat with the torch turned on

Walkie-talkies

2 torches (one for Anna, one for Suzanne)

A whistle

A compass

Biscuits

Life jacket

Snorkel

Camouflage

When the list was finished, Suzanne said we had too many things, and they would take too long to find. So we crossed the compass off because, like she said, we didn't know whether Joe's house was north or south or anything anyway. And we crossed off the life-jacket, and the snorkel, and the whistle as well. And Suzanne wanted to cross off the biscuits, too, but Tom said if we weren't taking biscuits he was staying at home, so I sneaked back into the house to get some. And I got two torches as well, one for me and one for Suzanne. And then we went in the garden, and smeared camouflage mud on our faces from Miss Matheson's flowerbed.

We got the Super-Speed-Bike-Machine out of the shed. And we walked it down the back lane. And Suzanne said we should have one last look at the New Rabbit, just in case. Because, like she said, there wasn't much point in going to rescue Joe, to bring him back to his rabbit, if it was already dead.

Suzanne shone her torch into the hutch. The New Rabbit opened its eyes, and groaned. I said maybe we should take the New Rabbit with us, in case it died while we were gone. And Suzanne said that was a good idea.

So I picked the New Rabbit up, and I wrapped Suzanne's coat around it. And I passed it to Tom,

in the trailer, to hold. The New Rabbit closed
its eyes. Tom held it close, and
stroked it behind the ears,
and spoke to it nice and
low.

And then Suzanne
said, 'Shh...' because
she had heard something.

I listened. There was a jingling
sound. I saw two yellow eyes, in the dark,
up the road. 'It's the Cat Attack Alarm!'
I said.

'Quick,' said Suzanne. 'Let's go.'

I got on the saddle of the Super-Speed-Bike-
Machine, and Suzanne got on the stunt pegs. And
the New Cat came nearer. And when it saw the
New Rabbit, it stared, and got down low, and its

eyes went very wide.

Suzanne looked at the map. 'Turn left!' she said.

I turned on the light. Tom held on tight, and Suzanne pushed off, and I started to pedal as fast as I could, and we all said, **'THREE, TWO, ONE, BLAST OFF!'**

And we went off, flying, down the hill, right in the middle of the road, because we were the only ones out. And we whizzed past the horse trough where Tom wets his wellies, and the shops, and the Bottom Bus Stop.

And Suzanne said, **'NOW WE'RE OUT OF BOUNDS!'**

And I rang the bell, and the wind made my eyes water, and Tom did the Batman song in the trailer in the back. And me and Suzanne got The Hysterics.

And when we came to the bridge, Suzanne said, 'Stop!' and she put her foot out, and I slammed on the brakes, because the traffic lights were on red.

We waited until the light went green. And we rode over the bridge. It was so quiet we could hear the river underneath. When we got to the roundabout, Suzanne said, 'Go left.'

And I did. Well, I *thought* I did, but I'm not very good with my left and my right. And roundabouts are hard.

"That's *right*," Suzanne said. 'Not right, *left!*'

'Left?'

'Right, yes!'

'Make up your mind!'

In the end we went round it about a million times. And Tom said he felt sick, and Suzanne told him to stop eating all the biscuits. And then she said, 'Anna, *here!*' And she grabbed the handlebars, and the Super-Speed-Bike-Machine turned, and we came off the roundabout, and hit a bit of gravel, and skidded, and the trailer hit a bump, and Tom and the New Rabbit and the trailer went flying, up in the air, and the trailer and Tom came down again with a thump.

And Tom said, 'Ouch.'

But he wasn't hurt because he said he was, 'saved by my Bob the Builder hard hat!'

'Where's the New Rabbit?' I said.

Tom looked down at his hands. It was gone.

Me and Suzanne got the walkie-talkies out.

We stood back to back. And Suzanne walked one way, and I walked the other, and we shone our torches from side to side.

'Suzanne to Anna. Suzanne to Anna. Come in, Anna. I'm at the gorse bush. What's your position? Over.'

'Anna to Suzanne. Anna to Suzanne. I'm at the traffic cone. Over.'

'Copy that. Traffic cone. Are you receiving me? Over.'

'Yes.'

Suzanne said, 'You're supposed to say, "Receiving you loud and clear".'

And I said, 'We haven't got time to do all the "Come ins", and the "Copies", and the "Over and outs" and all that. Let's just look for the New Rabbit!'

And then Suzanne started going on about her uncle again, and how he's in the army. And about how I shouldn't have wrapped the New Rabbit in her coat because she was cold, and if it was lost she would be in Big Trouble off her Dad.

And I said how losing someone's coat wasn't as bad as losing someone's rabbit, and what were we going to say to Joe-down-the-road? And then I saw something.

'Look. In the river!' I shone my torch on the water.

Me and Suzanne and Tom stood on the bank. Suzanne's coat floated past.

'Can rabbits swim?' Tom asked.

And me and Suzanne didn't answer, because

376

we both knew that they can't. And that the New Rabbit must have drowned. And Tom started to cry.

And I told him he was Batman and Bob the Builder, to try to make him stop. But he didn't. And he took his hard hat off, and put it on the ground.

And then Suzanne said, 'Shh, listen.' There was a jingling sound. It was coming from the bridge. There were two yellow eyes, in the dark, on the wall. 'It's the Cat Attack Alarm again.'

The New Cat came close, and it got down very low, and its eyes went very wide, and it stared at something near the edge of the river. And then it disappeared down the bank. And when it came back up, it was dragging something in its mouth. It dropped something white next to Tom's feet. I shone my torch on it. The white thing opened its eyes. They were pink.

'The New Rabbit!' Tom said. And he stopped crying, and stroked the New Cat on its head, until its ears went flat. And he gave it a biscuit. Which the New Cat didn't really like. And then the New Cat went back off over the bridge.

Tom got back in the trailer with the New Rabbit, and I sat on the saddle, and Suzanne stood on the stunt pegs. And Suzanne pushed off and I started to pedal. And we carried on down the track, on the Super-Speed-Bike-Machine, until we came to the old tunnel.

We went inside.

It was so dark in the tunnel, even with the

torches, that we couldn't see the sides.

Suzanne shouted, 'Hello…'

It echoed back, 'Hello… *low… low…* '

'Is there anybody there?' Suzanne said.

And the echo said, 'There… *ere… ere…*'

And we called out our names, and they echoed back, until we came out on the other side.

Suzanne looked at the map. 'We have to go over the field.'

We got off the Super-Speed-Bike-Machine, and hid it in the bushes.

Tom wasn't sure about going into the field because when we got near, we could see there were cows. And Tom doesn't like cows because he says they're too big. But I told Tom how cows never hurt anyone. And in the end Tom said okay.

We opened the big gate. And Suzanne held

the rabbit. And then we closed it again. Like the sign on it said.

And the cows turned to look at us, and one of them said, '**Mooo...**' but they didn't move.

The field was full of cowpats, and it was so muddy, it was hard to get across. And Tom's wellies kept getting stuck. When we got to the fence at the other side, Suzanne looked down at the map again.

'Over the stile,' she said.

And then, 'We're here.'

There were some buildings straight ahead. We looked at the picture that Joe had done. It matched. We counted the windows along to where Joe's bedroom was. And we threw stones up at it.

A light came on, and the curtains went back, and we saw Joe's face. The window opened.

I said, 'Hello, Joe.'

And Joe said, 'Who's that?'

Because it probably didn't look very like me because of the dark, and the cowpats, and the camouflage on my face and all that.

And I said, 'It's Anna.'

And Suzanne said, 'And Suzanne.'

And Tom said, 'And Tom.'

'We've come to rescue you,' said Suzanne.

Joe closed his window. And his curtains. And at first we thought he had gone back to bed. But then a door opened, downstairs.

Joe came out. And we told him all about how the New Rabbit had got poorly again, after he'd gone. And about the old couple in the paper, who got separated, and died of broken hearts. And about Suzanne's dream. And how the New Rabbit had screamed.

And Joe held the New Rabbit very close, and he put it inside his pyjama top, and he kissed it all over its face. And he said, 'Let's go home.'

And me and Tom and Suzanne and Joe walked through the gate, and started back across the field. Which Tom said he didn't mind this time because the cows had gone.

Until we got to the middle, when one appeared, right in front of us, in the dark.

'**Mooo . . .**' it said.

We stopped. The cow stared. And then another cow came, and another, and another.

I told Tom to ignore them.

Because
of how cows
had never hurt
anyone.

And I said,
'Isn't that right, Joe?'
Because Joe always
knows about things.

And Joe said how
that wasn't *exactly*
right because cows had hurt
some people, and once it was
someone who was walking his dog, and it was
definitely true because it was on the news, and
he was called Chris Pool.

And I said how they probably didn't hurt him
very badly, and it was probably only by mistake.

And Joe said how they had kicked him, and broken his ribs, and he was only saved because he was in the police and his friend rescued him in his helicopter. And if he hadn't the cows would have trampled him to death.

'Oh,' I said.

The cows came around us in a circle. And they rolled their eyes, and licked their lips. And I heard something roar, and at first I thought it was the noise cows make just before they trample you. So I closed my eyes.

But then I heard it again, and this time it sounded more like a car. So I opened my eyes. And I saw two headlights. And I heard a car horn. And I heard, 'Spot on, Skipper. Four sprogs. And they're surrounded. Got 'em in the old illuminators. Fall out.'

It was Mr Tucker. In his old sports car, wearing his driving goggles and his gloves. And Mrs Rotherham was with him.

Mrs Rotherham got out of the car, and she opened the gate, and then she got back in, and Mr Tucker drove the car right into the field and he flashed the lights and honked the horn. And Mrs Rotherham waved her walking stick. And the cows all scattered.

And Mr Tucker stopped the car and he said, 'Hallo, Basher.' And he gave Tom the salute.

And Tom gave Mr Tucker the salute back.

And Mr Tucker said, 'Hop in!'

And Tom got on Mr Tucker's knee, and Mr Tucker said, 'Bit of cowpat in the cockpit there, Basher.'

And the rest of us piled in the back.

And Mr Tucker said, 'Good God. Overload.'

And he put his goggles over his eyes and tightened his driving gloves and he said, 'Honk, honk!' Like Toad of Toad Hall does in my *Wind and the Willows* book at home.

And Mr Tucker drove us home even faster than the Super-Speed-Bike-Machine.

CHAPTER 17
The Poisoned Parsley

That was just about everything that happened in the Great Rabbit Rescue.

When we got home there were two police cars outside. Mum and Dad, and Suzanne's Mum and Dad, and Joe's Mum, and two policemen, were in our kitchen.

I thought we were in Big Trouble then, but nobody shouted, not even Suzanne's Dad. And Mum cuddled me and Tom in.

And Suzanne and her Mum and Dad went to their house.

And Joe and his Mum and the New Rabbit went to their house.

And the policemen filled in

their forms. And they went home as well.

And Mum made some tea for Mrs Rotherham. And Mr Tucker said he'd prefer something stronger. And Dad brought him some brandy. And Mr Tucker said, 'That's the ticket. Just a snifter.' And he drank it down in one.

And Mum made some hot milk for me and Tom. And Tom fell asleep on Mr Tucker's knee before his even came. And Mr Tucker fell asleep too. And he started snoring. And Mum and Mrs Rotherham got The Hysterics.

And then Mrs Rotherham told Mum the story of how her and Mr Tucker found us. And how she had seen the police cars, and come down the road, and how Mr Tucker was out, asking the police what was going on. And how the policemen said we were missing. And how Mrs Rotherham had seen the tyre tracks from the Super-Speed-Bike-Machine, at the bottom of the road, and that the hutch was open, and that the New Rabbit was gone, and how she went up to the shed, and saw all Joe's pictures about his rabbit, and the list about what he didn't like about living at his Dad's, and our plans on the wall, and how they had all been ticked off, except number four, which was, 'Rescue Joe Ourselves.'

And how she found the piece of paper with Joe's Dad's address. And how her and Mr Tucker tried to tell the police, but they said they had to take statements from everyone first. And how Mr Tucker said, 'Humph, Old Gendarmerie, load of old bull and bumph.' And got his old sports car out of the garage.

And that's all I remember, because then I fell asleep as well.

The next day, me and Suzanne and Tom and Joe stayed off school. And Joe came round in the morning to tell us that his Mum had taken the New Rabbit to the vet and how the vet had given the New Rabbit some pills, and said that the New Rabbit wasn't dying of a broken heart at all, it was dying because it had been poisoned.

And Suzanne said we had better do an investigation to find out who had poisoned it.

So we went to see Mrs Rotherham to ask her to help us, because of how she used to be in the police and everything.

And Suzanne said, 'Who could have done it?'

And Mrs Rotherham said, 'Who *indeed?*'

And she gave me and Suzanne a file with a label on it that said, 'The Case of the Poisoned Rabbit.' And inside it was our Spy Club notebook, which Mrs Rotherham had taken from the shed. And she had highlighted the bits about Joe going away, and about us feeding the New Rabbit, and the New Rabbit being unwell. And there were some privet leaves, and daffodil bulbs, and apple pips and some of the strange-smelling parsley from Miss Matheson's garden in the file as well. All in see-through plastic bags, sealed up. And they had tags on them that said, '*Evidence*'.

Digitalis

Foxglove

Hedera Helix
English
Common Ivy

391

And there was an old book with pictures of poisonous flowers and plants, and one of the corners of the pages was folded down. And on the page it said, 'Common house and garden plants toxic to Leporid creatures'. And all of the things in the little bags inside the file were on the list. And at the bottom of the list it said, '*Aethusa cynapium* or Fool's or Poison Parsley, easily distinguished from parsley proper by its height, girth and foul-smelling odour.'

Me and Suzanne looked up Leporid in my dictionary. It said . . .

Aethusa Cynapium
FOOLS PARSLEY

leporid [lep-uh-rid] ✦ *noun*
an animal of the family Leporidae, comprising
the rabbits and hares.

And we looked in Suzanne's as well. It said . . .

leporid [lep-uh-rid] ✦ *noun*
rabbit

The next day, at school, Joe sat back in his old
seat. And Mrs Peters called Joe's name out last on
the register. And Joe said, 'Here.'

Mrs Rotherham didn't tell anyone what had really
happened with Joe-down-the-road and his rabbit

and why it nearly died. And neither did me and Suzanne.

But we took the rest of the parsley out of the shed. And we put it on Miss Matheson's compost heap. And we hid the file of the Case of the Poisoned Rabbit next to the Spyclub Notebook, behind the worms, and the wasp trap, on the shelf in the shed.

Me and Suzanne don't go on the walkie-talkies as much anymore. Not now Joe is back down the road. Because mostly we play Dingo the Dog, and Mountain Rescue, and see how long we can stare at the sun before we go blind and all that.

We aren't allowed back on the Super-Speed-Bike-Machine though. Dad took me and Tom to find it, in the bushes, by the field by Joe's house. And when we got it home, and Mum saw how the stabilisers were hanging off, and the back wheel was bent, and one of the tyres had burst, she said, 'That contraption is condemned.'

And she tried to put it out with the bins.

But me and Tom begged, and in the end she let us put it back in the shed. Under the dust-sheet, behind the stepladders, and the garden canes and the broken old floorboards.

Suzanne says that when we're older, and we haven't got any bounds to be in, we can take the walkie-talkies as far away as we want. And one of us can go on the Super-Speed-Bike-Machine, and the other one can go on buses and boats and things like that.

And then Suzanne says she will say, 'Suzanne

to Anna. Suzanne to Anna. I'm in America. Are you receiving me? Over.'

And I will say, 'Anna to Suzanne. Anna to Suzanne. I'm in Afghanistan. Receiving you loud and clear. Over.'

Because those places are about the same far apartness from here. We've measured it on a map.

And, when we do it, I'm going to get Tom to come with me, and Suzanne is going to take Joe-down-the-road.

Because Tom and Joe love the Super-Speed-Bike-Machine, and buses, and boats and things like that. And they don't like being left behind.

The End

Katie Davies

Katie Davies was born in Newcastle Upon Tyne in 1978. In 1989, after a relentless begging campaign, she was given two Russian Dwarf hamsters by her Mum for Christmas. She is yet to recover from what happened to those hamsters. THE GREAT HAMSTER MASSACRE is Katie's first novel. She is currently working on its sequel, THE GREAT RABBIT RESCUE. Katie now lives in North London with her husband, the comedian Alan Davies, and their two children. She does not have any hamsters.

Hannah Shaw

Hannah Shaw was born into a large family of sprout-munching vegetarians. She spent her formative years trying to be good at everything; from roller-skating to gymnastics, but she soon realised there wasn't much chance of her becoming a gold medal winning gymnast, so she resigned herself to writing stories and drawing pictures instead!

Hannah currently lives in a little cottage in the Cotswolds, with her husband Ben the blacksmith and her rescue dog Ren. She finds her over-active imagination fuels new ideas but unfortunately keeps her awake at night!

Another great animal investigation from Katie Davies!

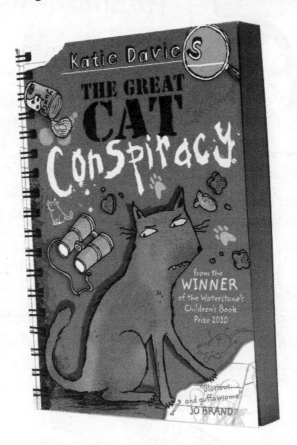

Available in all good bookshops.

The newest animal
investigation from Katie Davies!

Coming in June 2012!

www.katiedaviesbooks.com

Visit Katie Davies online and find out more amazing animal facts, fun activities and exclusive news...

HAMSTER SEARCH

Search for these words in the grid below. Words can read up, down, across, diagonally and backwards.

H	N	L	E	E	B	W
S	A	I	P	E	T	H
Q	K	M	B	A	A	I
U	A	B	S	B	I	S
E	E	C	P	T	L	K
A	U	A	A	C	E	E
L	Q	G	W	F	U	R
D	S	E	E	D	S	S

HAMSTER   PAW
WHISKERS   SQUEAK
NIBBLE   SEEDS
WHEEL   CAGE
SQUEAL   FUR
TAIL   PET

CROSSWORD Can you complete the crossword?

SHADOW PLAY

Which of these shadows exactly matches the pictured rabbit?

A   B   C
D   E   F

SPOT THE DIFFERENCE

Can you spot 5 differences in these pictures?

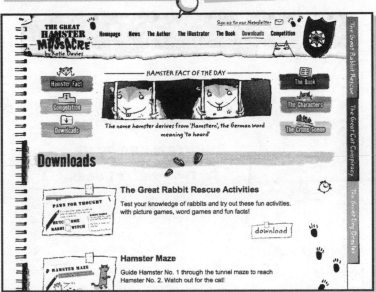

Hamster Fact
Competition
Downloads

— HAMSTER FACT OF THE DAY —

The name hamster derives from 'Hamstern', the German word meaning 'to hoard'

The Book
The Characters
The Crime Scene

Downloads

The Great Rabbit Rescue Activities

Test your knowledge of rabbits and try out these fun activities, with picture games, word games and fun facts!

download

Hamster Maze

Guide Hamster No. 1 through the tunnel maze to reach Hamster No. 2. Watch out for the cat!

AMAZING HAMSTER

Hamsters are excellent escapologists.

Hamsters are colour-blind.

Hamsters can only see up to six
inches in front of them.

 In the wild, a hamster's
burrow can be up
to two metres deep.

AND BUNNY FACTS!

The record for the longest ears on a rabbit stands with an American bunny, Nipper's Geronimo, whose ears measured a whopping 79 centimetres (31.125 inches).

A rabbit sweats through the pads on its feet.

Rabbits can see behind themselves without turning their heads.

A rabbit's teeth never stop growing.